"Don't Press Your Luck, Mr. Compton!"

Barrie stated firmly. "Don't you know it's dangerous to tamper with a starving woman? You promised me dinner, and all I've gotten so far is static."

"There is a certain amount of electricity in the air when we get together, isn't there?" Michael murmured softly. Barrie flushed under the intensity of his gaze and tried not to notice how well his designer jeans hugged his thighs.

"That wasn't what I meant," she countered unconvincingly.

"Maybe not," he said, with a definite twinkle in his eye. "But it's true. Maybe we should explore the idea a bit after dinner."

Dessert, she thought. Michael thought *she* was on the menu for dessert. Barrie swallowed and faced him. Maybe if she kept her mind on the appetizers, she wouldn't feel quite so panicky about dessert....

Dear Reader,

Welcome to Silhouette! Our goal is to give you hours of unbeatable reading pleasure, and we hope you'll enjoy each month's six new Silhouette Desires. These sensual, provocative love stories are both believable and compelling—sometimes they're poignant, sometimes humorous, but always enjoyable.

Indulge yourself. Experience all the passion and excitement of falling in love along with our heroine as she meets the irresistible man of her dreams and together they overcome all obstacles in the path to a happy ending.

If this is your first Desire, I hope it'll be the first of many. If you're already a Silhouette Desire reader, thanks for your support! Look for some of your favorite authors in the coming months: Stephanie James, Diana Palmer, Dixie Browning, Ann Major and Doreen Owens Malek, to name just a few.

Happy reading!

Isabel Swift
Senior Editor

SDRL-7/85

SHERRYL WOODS
Not at Eight, Darling

Silhouette Desire

Published by Silhouette Books New York

America's Publisher of Contemporary Romance

SILHOUETTE BOOKS
300 East 42nd St., New York, N.Y. 10017

Copyright © 1986 by Sherryl Woods

ISBN: 0-373-05309-6

First Silhouette Books printing October 1986

America's Publisher of Contemporary Romance

Printed in the U.S.A.

SHERRYL WOODS

lives by the ocean, which provides daily inspiration for the romance in her soul. Her years as a television critic taught her about steamy plots and humor. Her years as a travel editor took her to exotic locations. Her years as a crummy weekend tennis player taught her to stick with what she enjoyed most: writing. What better way to combine all of that than by writing romantic stories about wonderful heroines, sensitive heroes and enchanting locations?

One

The only sound in the hushed, cavernous television studio was the increasingly rapid, evidently angry tapping of Barrie MacDonald's pen against the metal top of a makeshift conference table. Then, as a dozen people looked on in anxious and surprisingly silent anticipation, she dropped the memo she'd been reading, peered over the top of her oversized glasses with indignant brown eyes and spoke in a voice that, she noted proudly, was quiet and controlled. It was not at all like the scream of pure frustration she wanted to unleash on poor, unsuspecting Kevin Porterfield.

"Kevin, dear, did you read this?"

The young man gulped nervously. "Of course, Miss MacDonald."

"Then you know how utterly absurd it is," she said softly. She actually sounded calm. Amazing. "I will not add a sheepdog to the cast of *Goodbye, Again*, just because some crazy demographic study shows that kids like sheepdogs."

Several members of the cast gasped as eyebrows lifted toward the ceiling in a disgusted, what-did-you-expect expression. Others simply giggled. If the memo hadn't sounded so incredibly serious, Barrie might have laughed herself. Instead she managed an expression she hoped would put the fear of God into this...this Yuppie who was still wet behind the ears and who was staring at her now with a look that teetered between misery and smug satisfaction. It was actually a rather amazing combination, and she wondered for a fleeting second how he managed it. If he could do it on command, he might make a decent actor.

"But Miss MacDonald..." he began again.

"That's all there is to it, Kevin," she interrupted firmly. "End of discussion."

"But Miss MacDonald, I'm afraid Mr. Compton was adamant. The show has to have a dog. The research shows that dogs..."

"I know what the bloody research shows, Kevin," she said, her voice beginning to rise toward a less-than-serene screech, despite her best efforts to control it. She took a deep, relaxing breath—precisely as she'd learned in her stress reduction class—and added more gently, "If the research showed that viewers liked ax murders, would you expect me to put one of those in each week, too?"

Kevin looked at her indignantly. "Of course not."

"Then don't talk to me about research. Have you read the script for this show, Kevin? We are talking adult situation comedy here. We are talking relationships. Funny, sophisticated relationships. We are not talking dog food commercials."

Poor Kevin turned absolutely pale, but Barrie was not about to relent and let him off the hook. She had created *Goodbye, Again*. It was her statement about the transitory nature of romance in the 80s, about her values. There was an awful lot of her in the single, independent, fiesty heroine. Each time Karen Devereaux spoke, Barrie felt as though it was an echo of her own thoughts. *Goodbye, Again* had been born of her beliefs, and she had spent three long, agonizing years trying to get it on the air. She was not about to let these mindless, research-oriented twits destroy it on the first day of production. If she gave in on the dog, next week they'd want to add kids, and the week after that her lead character would be married and pregnant, and there would be a whole disgustingly cheery episode revolving around diapers and baby food. Well, they could take their blasted market research and stuff it!

Aloud, she said none of this. Exercising what she considered to be Emmy-Award-winning restraint, she murmured pleasantly, "Now you run along and explain that to Mr. Compton, dear. I'm sure he'll understand."

"Understand what?"

The question, asked in a low, velvet-smooth tone, came from the back of the studio. It was exactly the sort of warm, soothing, sensual voice that radio stations liked to have on the air in the wee hours of the morning to stir the imagination of their female listeners. Despite her instinctive, sinking feeling that the voice belonged to Michael Compton, Barrie's own heart lurched at the seductive sound. Then it had a far more sensible reaction. It slammed against her ribs in sheer panic.

Michael Compton, the recently appointed network vice president for programming, was a man who reportedly dissected into tiny, insignificant pieces the people who dared to question his orders. Barrie wondered how much of her conversation with Kevin he'd overheard. Not that she'd change a word of it, she thought stoutly. It would just be nice to know exactly how much trouble she was in.

She had to admit that the man's timing was impeccable. "Just when I've got the battle under control, the enemy general has to show up with reinforcements," she muttered resignedly under her breath.

She should have anticipated something like this. The day had not gone well since the alarm clock had jarred her awake at daybreak. In fact, on a scale of one to ten, it ranked somewhere on the minus side of the ledger. First she had inadvertently washed one of her new soft contact lenses down the drain, leaving her to choose between blinking nearsightedness or the huge old rose-tinted glasses that made her look a bit like an owl. Then her hairdryer had sparked and sizzled to an abrupt halt, leaving her frosted ash-brown hair to dry naturally to a curly tangle, rather than the smoother style she preferred. Her windshield wipers had broken in the middle of a downpour, and she'd had to creep along the L.A. freeway, arriving at the studio an hour late. And finally, she had snagged her new hose as she was getting out of her sporty fire-engine-red Sentra in the parking lot. The run had made its way from her ankle to her thigh in less time than it had taken her to utter a satisfying string of obscenities under her breath.

"Apparently I'm on a roll," she said dryly as the man whom she assumed to be Michael Compton stepped out of the shadows and strolled confidently to the temporary office set of *Goodbye, Again*, where Barrie and the cast were assembled. They had been rehearsing the premiere episode when Kevin had wandered in with the latest memo from the network.

"Well, Miss MacDonald," the man said, a hint of amusement twinkling in his eyes as he perched on the edge of the conference table right next to her. One very solid, very tempting thigh was mere inches from her fingertips. "Exactly what is it you're so sure I'll understand?"

Barrie's gaze shifted reluctantly upward into dazzling blue-green eyes. She studied the square jaw and the determined set to his mouth and gulped. Perhaps a dog wouldn't be so bad, after all. He could stay in the bedroom and bark occasionally. That ought to keep everyone happy.

What in God's name am I thinking of? she snapped back mentally. I will not have a dog in this show!

Staring him straight in the eye, she said coolly, "We were just discussing your memo, Mr. Compton."

"About the sheepdog."

"Yes. I'm not sure you've thought this through," she began cautiously, wincing as his eyes hardened and bored into her. Mincemeat. This was definitely a man who made mincemeat out of his adversaries. She rushed on, anyway. If she was going to commit professional suicide, she might as well go out fighting. "I mean these people live in a thirty-five story condominium in the middle of Manhattan. What would they be doing with a sheepdog?"

"That's something else we need to talk about," he said.

Although he spoke softly, there was no mistaking the authoritative tone. A warning signal flared in Barrie's brain, and she prepared for the next wave of his absurd, ill-conceived game plan to destroy her show.

"I don't think a condominium is quite the right environment," he explained.

"Oh? And what would you suggest? A vine-covered cottage with a white picket fence?"

He grinned, and her own lips defied her by twitching upward in an involuntary response. "That might be a little extreme," he agreed. "I was thinking more along the lines of a town house."

Barrie considered the idea thoughtfully. She was not above making some small compromises. "Maybe it would work," she said slowly. "One of those nice brownstones on the East Side, perhaps."

"Umm..." He shook his head. "Not exactly."

"What, then?"

"I was thinking of one of those town house developments. You know, with a swimming pool, tennis courts, sailboats, that sort of thing."

Barrie's eyes widened incredulously. The man had obviously come up through the ranks from sales. He had the creative mentality of an accountant.

"In Manhattan?" That distressing screech was back in her voice, though it had been weakened considerably by her absolute dismay.

"Well, we probably would have to move the location of the show. Maybe Marina del Ray or Santa Monica."

At that, her mouth dropped open, and her glasses slipped to the tip of her pert turned-up nose. "You've got to be kidding!"

"What's wrong with that? It worked for *Three's Company*."

To her thorough astonishment, the man seemed genuinely puzzled. In fact, he looked downright hurt that she hadn't liked his suggestion.

"That's what's wrong with it," she explained as patiently as she could, considering her desire to deliver a primal scream that would shake the studio. "It's been done. I don't want to copy another series. *Goodbye, Again* is going to be fresh, different, contemporary. It's going to give viewers something to think about."

She glared at him defiantly. "It is not going to be an endless parade of bikini-clad bodies jiggling to the Jacuzzi."

"You think that's a bit too sexist?" he wondered aloud with apparent innocence. While she held her breath and waited, he seemed to consider her strenuous objection carefully. "Maybe you're right. Of course, if we put a couple of guys in there..."

"Forget it!" Barrie's shout echoed as she slammed her fist down emphatically. To her utter chagrin it landed squarely on his thigh. The damn muscle felt like granite. It felt, in fact, wonderful. However, she warned herself dryly, this was no time to get caught up with the feel of the man's physique. She had an important point to make. Several of them, in fact. "No bikinis! No swimming pools! And no damned sheepdog!"

A deep, rumbling laugh suddenly erupted from Michael Compton's chest. Barrie's hand twitched nervously where it had come to rest on his leg, and she yanked it back, looking at him as though he'd suddenly gone mad. The cast tittered uncertainly.

"You're wonderful, Miss MacDonald. Absolutely priceless," he said when he'd regained his composure. "I like a producer with spunk. I want my people to stand up for what they believe in."

His people? Spunk? Barrie's indignant roar dwindled down to a low growl as she stared at him, first in blinking confusion, then with slowly dawning understanding. "You were teasing me, weren't you?" she accused.

"Me?" The attempt at innocence failed miserably. There was far too much of a twinkle in his eyes.

"Yes, you."

He nodded contritely, though his lips continued to twitch with amusement. "I'm afraid so. I couldn't resist."

"You don't want me to move the show to Los Angeles?"

He shook his head.

"You don't expect me to spend five minutes per episode in a Jacuzzi?"

"Nope."

"You're not really asking for a sheepdog?"

"Well..."

"Mr. Compton," she thundered.

He smiled at her. Slowly. Winningly. It was a smile that belonged on the cover of an album of romantic ballads. "Okay, you win. No sheepdog...if you have dinner with me."

Despite the flutter in the pit of her stomach, Barrie refused to be won over. "Business conferences usually take place over lunch."

"I'm booked for lunch for the next month."

"I'll wait."

"I won't. If this show is going to go on the air in September—three weeks from now, in fact—we need to discuss it."

Barrie regarded him closely, one eyebrow lifting quizzically. "Mr. Compton," she began sweetly. "Are you blackmailing me into having dinner with you?"

"Miss MacDonald, do I look like I need to blackmail women into going out with me?" he inquired with entirely too much amusement.

Barrie surveyed him critically from head to toe and decided reluctantly that the amusement didn't stem from conceit. If anything, the man was probably being modest. Her gaze traveled slowly from the neatly trimmed thick brown hair and twinkling blue-green eyes over broad shoulders and narrow hips that not even a depressingly businesslike navy blue suit could disguise. The Kirk Douglas dimple in his chin and the square jaw only added to his aura of sex appeal. To top it off, he apparently had charm, and he definitely had power, both potent aphrodisiacs.

No, she decided with an unconscious sigh, this man would not need to resort to blackmail. Women probably lined up hoping for a chance to have him as an escort. Her glance swept over the cast of *Goodbye, Again*. Although they all seemed to be nervously awaiting her decision, disgustingly the women also appeared to be panting. Any one of them would probably kill to trade places with her.

"Well?" he taunted. "Are you going to take me up on this opportunity to discuss your future at the network?"

"Don't rush me. I'm thinking," she retorted, deliberately ignoring the ominous overtone of his question.

"If it takes you this long to reach a decision, Miss MacDonald, perhaps you've chosen the wrong career. Producers need to think on their feet."

"Perhaps I could become a network vice president," she suggested darkly. "They don't seem to think at all."

To her absolute amazement—and probable salvation—he laughed again. Her eyes widened as the hearty, unrestrained sound bounced off the studio walls. "Watch it, Miss MacDonald," he warned with a wink as he headed toward the door with Kevin trailing along behind him like an obedient puppy. "Casting has a huge sheepdog that would be just perfect for this show."

Barrie winced and took a deep breath. "Pick me up here at seven," she called after him.

With her glasses clenched tightly in her hand, Barrie couldn't quite see to the back of the studio, but Michael appeared to nod in satisfaction. "Six-thirty. My office," he called back as the door slammed shut behind him.

"Smart . . ." she muttered under her breath.

She hated men who had to have the last word. She especially hated men who had irresistible thighs.

Two

The studio was silent for exactly thirty seconds following Michael Compton's departure. Then all hell broke loose. Though Barrie would have liked to believe they were above it, the women immediately—and probably predictably—began debating the man's availability amid a chorus of heavy sighs. At the same time, the men's grumbling remarks about interference in the creative process by self-important pompous jerks contained more than a hint of jealousy. The writer of the opening episode muttered something about cretins under his breath, while he crushed empty Styrofoam coffee cups one by one. And Danielle Lawrence, Barrie's best friend and the director whom she'd chosen for the series' premiere, was ignoring all of it and smirking at her.

"What's your problem?" Barrie snapped.

"Nice looking, isn't he?"

"Who?" It seemed to be a good time to be deliberately obtuse.

"Who? Attila the programmer, of course."

"I didn't notice."

Danielle regarded her skeptically. "The woman who has taken a personal oath not to marry until she finds the perfect set of male thighs did not notice a man whose legs could have been carved by Michelangelo? I find that difficult to believe."

Barrie's eyes flashed dangerously. "There are other directors in Hollywood."

"But I'm good," Danielle retorted cheerfully. "I am also available, reasonably inexpensive, and I know all of your character flaws and love you, anyway. You can't top that."

Barrie sighed. "You're probably right, but could we drop the subject of Michael Compton for now? We have to go over this opening scene again. The pacing is all wrong."

An explosion of sound erupted just behind Barrie's shoulder. "What do you mean the pacing is all wrong?" Heath Donaldson hissed. "I've been writing comedy since before you were born. If you'd hired actors who knew how to deliver a line, the pacing would be just fine."

Barrie rolled her eyes at Danielle and turned around slowly. She put her arm around the short balding man who'd been huffing and puffing angrily in her ear. "Sweetheart," she began soothingly. "Your script is just fine. We all know you're one of the best in the business.''

She lowered her voice to a whisper. ''And you're right about some of the cast being inexperienced. But, love, you know they're just perfect for the parts. I think if you work with them and make just a few tiny adjustments to help them out, the opening scene will click right along.''

Heath blinked back at her, and the fiery red that had crept up his neck was fading away. He now looked a little less like a coronary waiting to happen. Barrie breathed a sigh of relief as he muttered more calmly, ''Well, I suppose I could change a few lines just a little, tighten it up.''

''That's it,'' Barrie said with exaggerated enthusiasm. ''I knew you could do it. Why don't you and Danielle go over the first couple of pages of the script and see what you can come up with?''

For the next few hours Barrie felt like a firefighter who'd been asked to put out an entire county of brush fires with a pail of water. There was one crisis after another, none of them serious, but all of them requiring diplomacy, patience and a serenity she was far from feeling. The only possible advantage to a day like today, she decided, rubbing her throbbing temples, was that it had left her absolutely no time to work herself into a state over her impending dinner with Michael Compton.

At six-fifteen she sent the cast and crew home, touched up her makeup, took another stress-reducing deep breath that didn't do a bit of good and walked across the studio lot to the nearby network facilities.

At precisely six-thirty she presented herself to Michael Compton's secretary, a cheerful woman with gray hair, rosy cheeks and sparkling, periwinkle blue eyes.

Mrs. Emma Lou Hastings looked as though she'd be perfectly at home in the kitchen making applesauce with an army of grandchildren underfoot. She also seemed like the type you could come to for motherly advice, Barrie decided, suddenly struck by the oddest desire to sit down and tell this perfect stranger that she was a nervous wreck because she was having dinner with a man who held the key to her future, a man who also had incredible thighs. She wondered what Mrs. Hastings would have to say about that.

Since Barrie kept her mouth clamped firmly shut, Mrs. Hastings only said, "You can go in now, Miss MacDonald. Mr. Compton is expecting you."

Barrie had started toward the door when the secretary added softly, "Don't worry, dear. He's really a very nice young man."

Very nice young man, indeed! Mrs. Hastings obviously didn't know that Michael Compton had virtually threatened to cancel Barrie's series unless she agreed to this dinner. What would she say about her nice young man if she found out about that? Barrie looked into her round, honest-looking face with the tiny laugh lines around the eyes and the encouraging smile and didn't have the heart to tell her. After all, she defended herself, could you tell a mother that her son is rotten to the core? Of course not. No more than she could tell Mrs. Hastings that her obviously well-liked boss was a thoroughly obnoxious louse who indulged in emotional blackmail.

Instead she smiled back. "Thanks," she said as she turned the brass doorknob and walked into Michael Compton's office. Grateful for any reprieve, she was delighted to see that he was on the phone. He looked up and grinned at her with that sinfully sensual smile of his and motioned for her to sit down. She selected the chair farthest from his desk and sank down, tucking her legs back in a futile attempt to cover the run that displayed a pale white trail of skin from her ankle up, disappearing at last under the hem of her beige linen skirt. Why the hell hadn't she remembered the damn run earlier? She couldn't very well go tearing out of here now to buy new hose. Blast Michael Compton, she thought irrationally. Somehow this was all his fault.

She glanced over to discover that the object of her irritation was paying absolutely no attention to her. His head was bent to one side in order to keep the phone braced against his shoulder. If he did that long enough, he was going to have one heck of a neck ache, Barrie noted. She was torn between a perverse delight at the prospect and an even stranger desire to massage the soon-to-be-knotted muscles. She blinked and looked away, but, as though she'd been hypnotized, her eyes were drawn back time and again.

As Michael listened to his long-winded and apparently irate caller, he tapped a pencil idly on his huge rosewood desk. With his other hand he shuffled through a stack of papers, sorting them into two compulsively neat piles. Periodically he jabbed at another of the lit buttons on the phone, rumbled directives first into the receiver and then into the intercom on his desk. Two assistants scurried in and out, handing him papers to sign, waiting as he jotted notes on them, then rushing back out. A clerk from the mailroom came in with a half-dozen videotapes, piled them up next to his VCR and the bank of television monitors and left. Mrs. Hastings hurried in with several bulging file folders, dropped them into his In basket and picked up one of the stacks he'd just created. On her way out, she smiled sympathetically at Barrie, who'd begun to feel as though she'd fallen into the rabbit hole and wound up in the middle of *Alice in Wonderland*. Never in her life had she seen such perfectly orchestrated chaos. Never in her life had she felt so blatantly ignored.

"It won't be long, dear," Mrs. Hastings promised. "It's always this way at the end of the day."

Barrie glanced at her slim gold watch. It was seven-fifteen. She had suggested that Michael meet her at the studio at seven, but he'd refused and insisted instead that she meet him at his office at six-thirty. He was now forty-five minutes late, and Mrs. Hastings's reassurances to the contrary, he was showing no sign of quitting for the day.

Barrie waited and fumed. Eager to find any excuse for escape, she prepared herself mentally to rise as regally as she could with that blasted run in her hose and walk out of his office in a dignified protest of his imperious rudeness. Just as she started to stand, the phone clicked into place on his desk. He dropped the pencil, stopped shuffling papers, switched off the intercom and leaned back in his chair.

His pale blue tailored-to-fit shirt with his initials embroidered on the cuff emphasized his broad chest, his tapering waistline. His tie was loosened, his collar open at the neck to reveal a provocative amount of tanned skin and a shadowing of dark, tightly curled hairs. Eyes that now seemed more blue than green stared knowingly back at her. Barrie gulped and studied the pictures on the wall. They were modern splashes of bright, formless color. They were awful.

"So...Miss MacDonald," he said softly, seductively. "What do you think of my—" there was a suggestive hesitation that brought a guilty blush to Barrie's cheeks "—office?"

"I think the network overpaid the decorator," she responded tartly.

He grinned at her. "That's a rather dangerously blunt comment, don't you think? How do you know I didn't do it myself?"

"I've been in this office before. The pictures preceded you."

"Very observant," he noted approvingly, then added with a weary sigh, "I wish more people in this business would develop their powers of observation. It might improve the quality of the stuff that gets brought in here."

Barrie's brown eyes sparkled with excitement as she recognized a perfect opportunity. Heath Donaldson couldn't have scripted a better opening line for her. "That's what I want to do with *Goodbye, Again*," she said enthusiastically. "I want to create characters and situations that people will recognize. Relationships today aren't what they were when *I Love Lucy* went on the air. They're freer, more open. Women are less dependent on the men in their lives, married or not. They stay married out of choice, not necessity. How many families today are like the Andersons on *Father Knows Best*? We might wish they were, but, as the saying goes, wishing won't make it so.''

"So you want to force-feed reality, when what the audience wants is fantasy?'' he challenged.

"No,'' she responded heatedly, so caught up in explaining her show so that he would understand that she once again missed the teasing glint in his eyes. "You're twisting my words around. You make reality sound like a dirty word.''

As Michael rose and walked slowly around to where she was sitting, her breath suddenly caught in her throat, her argument sputtered to a halt, and she was immediately struck by the strangest sense of heightened anticipation. It was like waiting for a roller coaster to inch over the crest of its highest peak and fly down the other side. One knew something incredible was about to happen but had no idea quite how to prepare for it. Michael's impressive body towered over hers, sending out little electrical currents that seemed to head straight for her abdomen, flooding it with a pleasant warmth and a tormenting ache. Barrie's eyes were drawn to his, locked in a fiery awareness, challenging him to defend his statement.

"Actually, I like reality, Miss MacDonald,'' he protested softly, the velvet-smooth tone affecting her like warm brandy. It felt soothing and intoxicating. "In fact, I'm liking it more by the minute."

His charming, roguish grin brought a responding tilt to her lips. The man could obviously sweet-talk his way past Saint Peter at the gates of heaven. What possible chance did she stand, Barrie wondered a trifle desperately. She'd come here to have a serious discussion to assure the integrity of *Goodbye, Again*, and here she was melting like some damned stick of butter left out in the sun. Spineless. She was absolutely spineless.

"Mr. Compton, I thought you wanted to have dinner and talk about *Goodbye, Again*."

"I do."

"Well?"

"Dinner's on the way."

Barrie gulped. "Here?"

"Why not? It's more private than a restaurant, and despite the lousy artwork, the atmosphere isn't bad."

It is also entirely too intimate, Barrie wanted to shout.

So what? a voice shouted back. Intimacy is only threatening if you allow it to be. After all, the man has done absolutely nothing to indicate that he wants to seduce you. That was an idea that popped into your mind sometime between his thorough, unblinking survey and the soft, sensual smile that made your heart flip over.

Okay. So I'll force that idea right back out of my mind.

Right. The worst thing that could happen would be that he'd make a pass at you, and you'd file a sexual harassment suit.

No, she correctly dryly, the worst thing that could happen would be that he would make a pass, and she would respond. She steeled herself against that embarrassingly distinct possibility.

"Dinner here is just fine," she said airily, taking off her glasses. Maybe if she couldn't see the man, his potency would be less dangerous. Of course, she also might miss the first signs of any planned seduction. She put the glasses back on, just in time to see a waiter wheel in a cart laden with covered silver dishes.

In less time than it would normally take her to scan the contents of her virtually empty freezer, the waiter draped a small table with a spotless white damask cloth, added an Oriental-style arrangement of tiny orchids, lit several tapered candles and set two places with heavy silverware and English bone china that Barrie recognized as one of the most expensive patterns on the market.

"I take it you didn't order from the commissary," she commented dryly.

He smiled back at her. "Wait until you see the food before making judgments, Miss MacDonald," he warned. "Isn't Hollywood known for creating atmosphere without worrying about substance? You could be in for a dinner of ham on rye."

"You don't strike me as the ham-on-rye type. Maybe bologna."

"Careful. That tart tongue of yours is going to get you in trouble yet."

"It usually gets me back out of it, as well."

"Perhaps it has...in the past," he taunted. "But you haven't come up against a man like me before, Miss MacDonald."

"How do you know that?"

"I'm one of a kind," he informed her with a wink as he sipped the wine and nodded approvingly to the waiter. "This is perfect, Henri."

"*Bon appetit, monsieur.*"

"*Merci.*"

The waiter bowed graciously to Barrie and pushed the cart out of the office, leaving them alone.

"Well, Miss MacDonald," Michael said softly as he held out a chair for her. "Your dinner awaits."

Barrie sat down to a meal that was expertly planned, perfectly prepared and, despite Michael's warnings, quite obviously not commissary fare. It began with pâté and ended with fresh strawberries and thick, sweet Devon cream, each course a sensual delight.

Their conversation throughout was surprisingly light and witty. In fact, on several occasions Barrie had the feeling she was caught up in the middle of a briskly paced Noel Coward script. Never had she met anyone who could match wits with her so easily, who could make her feel so much like a woman while at the same time treating her as an equal. It was exactly the sort of relationship she hoped to create on *Goodbye, Again*, straightforward, intelligent, lively and provocative. Ah, yes, she thought with an unconscious sigh. Most definitely provocative.

As the meal ended at last, she was savoring one of the strawberries, slowly licking the cream from its sweet tip before taking the bright red berry into her mouth, when she noticed that Michael seemed fascinated with her lips. His eyes sparkled as he licked his own lips in unconscious imitation of her actions. Stunned by the obvious sensuality of his response and heady from the fine wine and the unexpected knowledge that she could stir him as he did her, Barrie almost involuntarily prolonged the moment, biting into the juicy strawberry with slow deliberation. A husky moan rumbled deep in Michael's throat, and at last he blinked and looked away.

My God, what am I doing? The thought ripped into Barrie's mind, and she practically swallowed the strawberry whole. She had been taunting Michael Compton, practically daring him to respond to her as a woman. He did not strike her as the type to back away from a challenge, and she had just presented him with a practically irresistible one. I must be out of my mind.

"About *Goodbye, Again*," she prompted in a voice that had a distressing quiver in it. Damn! All those acting classes, and she still couldn't hide her nervousness.

"Why don't we sit over here and talk about it?" he suggested agreeably, leading her to a sofa and then sitting down entirely too near to her.

She studied him closely and promptly projected her wayward thoughts onto him. "Is this the part where you tell me you'll cooperate with me, if I *cooperate* with you?" she asked, actually managing a lightly teasing tone, despite the fact that her blood was roaring in her ears like an erupting volcano. In anger? Or anticipation? She wasn't at all sure and, disgustingly, he only seemed to find her implication amusing.

"No. This is the part where I tell you what's going to happen to your series."

"And?"

"And you tell me you're a professional, and you can handle the changes I'm demanding."

Changes? Demanding? She had the distinct impression he had deliberately chosen those words just to unnerve her. Well, she was not too proud to admit—to herself—that he'd succeeded. For his benefit, she plastered an interested, calm expression on her face and asked quietly, "What did you have in mind?"

"For one thing, I've been taking a look at the fall schedule, and I don't think it's as competitive as it could be. In order to make it more effective, I'm going to move your show."

Barrie eyed him cautiously. "Yes?"

"I think it'll be perfect for the eight o'clock slot on Saturday."

All attempts at studied tranquility flew out the window. Barrie's protest began as a small grumble, but by the time it exploded from her mouth it was a full-blown roar of incredulous frustration. "Michael . . . I mean, Mr. Compton, no! You can't do this!"

"Oh, yes, I can," he said evenly.

Of course he could. She took a very deep breath and decided to appeal to his sense of logic. "I'm not sure you realize what a risk you're taking. You could kill the show. This program is targeted for young adults. Young adults do not watch television at eight on a

Saturday night. Kids watch television at eight on Saturday."

"That's right. But I'm betting that the right show can keep some of those young adults hanging around home a little later. If it's good enough," he said slowly, throwing down the gauntlet, "they'll watch it while they get ready to go out." He paused to let that sink in, then added pointedly, "They watched Mary Tyler Moore on Saturday nights."

Mary Tyler Moore, indeed! They didn't even bring *her* back on Saturday night. Barrie's eyes were flashing, their usual soft brown shade glinting with sparks like flaming firewood. "Are you challenging me?"

He chuckled at her reaction. "You bet I am. Think you're up to it?" he asked softly, his eyes meeting hers with a question that had nothing to do with challenges and everything to do with romance and the very real male-female pull that had been playing tug-of-war with them since the moment they met.

A perfectly manicured, very masculine finger reached out to the tear in her hose and slowly traced the path it had taken from ankle to knee.

Barrie gasped softly. "Now we get to the part where you ask for my cooperation," she murmured shakily, fighting the heat that had swept through her at his touch.

He shook his head. "Not everything in this business comes down to sex."

She glanced down at his hand, which was still resting lightly, provocatively on her leg. "I wonder where I got the idea that it did?"

He chuckled and removed his hand. "Oh, I want you, Barrie MacDonald. I'm not about to deny it. I've wanted you since the first moment I saw you in that studio this afternoon. We're two of a kind, and I think we'd be very good together."

He paused to let his words sink in. Barrie gulped, wet her lips and waited breathlessly for what was to come. She couldn't have managed two sensible words had her life depended on it.

"But I won't ever ask anything of you that you're not prepared to offer," he promised in a voice that tantalized her with its rough huskiness. "And it will never have anything to do with *Goodbye, Again.*"

He paused again, and his blue-green eyes locked with hers. Finally, after several long seconds in which Barrie could feel each contraction of her pounding heart, he asked softly, "Do you believe me?"

Oddly, despite her thundering heartbeat and the wildfire that blazed through her, heating her blood to a glorious warmth, she did believe him. She believed she could trust him. She certainly believed he wanted her. And she also knew with absolute certainty that she'd better get the hell out of there before she made him that offer he'd just sworn to wait for.

"I think I'd better be going," she announced firmly.

"Stay."

She shook her head. "I can't."

"Can't? Or won't?"

"Does it matter? I'm leaving?"

"Okay, producer lady," he said quietly, surprising Barrie with his complete lack of anger, his ready capitulation. "If that's what you have to do. But I'll be in touch."

"I'm sure," Barrie said dryly. "You'll probably decide you want that sheepdog in the show, after all."

"Now that you mention it . . ."

"Forget it, buster," she said emphatically, unable to prevent the small grin that tugged at her mouth and softened the effect of her vehemence. "Heath Donaldson is going to flip out when he hears about the time change. If I have to tell him to incorporate a sheepdog, as well, he'll quit faster than you can say demographics."

"In that case, I'll hold off on the sheepdog . . . for a few days," he said, his eyes taking on the sort of caressing, speculative masculine gleam that usually precedes a kiss.

"Good night, Mr. Compton," Barrie said firmly, ducking past his descending head.

"Good night, Barrie MacDonald." The words were softly spoken and tinged with tolerant amusement.

As she walked to the elevator, Barrie wondered idly what it would be like to hear those perfectly innocuous, ordinary words murmured in her ear as she fell asleep each night. Probably wonderful. She pressed the Down button and leaned weakly against the wall while she waited.

MacDonald, you are crazy. Certifiably insane! You are going to get yourself in over your head on this one yet. She shook her head. Going to? Lady, the water's already up to your eyebrows!

Three

_____

The door to Barrie's tiny nondescript office crashed open at barely 8:00 a.m., and Danielle breezed in with a paper bag in one hand and her script in the other. She tossed the script into a chair, took two cups of coffee and two gooey sweetrolls from the bag and arranged them neatly on the desk, then sat down on the sofa with her jeans-clad legs crossed under her and stared at Barrie expectantly.

"Well?"

"Don't you ever knock?"

"Rarely," she retorted easily, obviously not the least bit put off by Barrie's grumpiness. "Why are you in such a snit? Didn't your dinner with the scrumptious Michael Compton go well?"

"Dinner was just fine," Barrie admitted honestly. "The problem came after dinner."

Danielle's gray eyes immediately narrowed. "Ohhh..." she began softly. Then her voice heated up angrily. "Why, the absolute gall of that man! Did he come on to you? File charges. That's what you should do. File charges. You can't let him get away with that."

"Whoa! You sound like an ambulance chaser. Do you have an attorney someplace who needs a case?" Barrie responded, chuckling at her friend's immediate rush to her defense. She reassured her, "It was nothing like that."

"He didn't come on to you?" Danielle's tone teetered between disappointment and skepticism.

Barrie's expression softened as she recalled in precise and blood-stirring detail Michael's almost casual advances, his seductive promises. "I wouldn't say that exactly," she admitted. "But it wasn't like what you meant."

"You mean you liked it."

"No, I didn't like it," Barrie said defensively. "I mean, it was okay. Oh, I don't know what I mean."

"He got to you, didn't he?" Danielle said triumphantly. "I knew it. I knew you wouldn't be able to resist those thighs."

"Damn it, Dani, it is not what you think!" There was an almost plaintive note in her protest. Michael Compton was the network vice president for programming, her boss, and that was all. It had to be. She was not going to let Danielle or her own skittering pulse rate tell her otherwise.

"Then what was the problem?"

"He's moving the show to eight o'clock on Saturday," she said in a rush of words, grateful to change the subject to one she knew would completely distract Danielle from her pursuit of the intimate details of her dinner with Michael.

Her announcement had the desired effect. Danielle was clearly shocked. "You can't be serious!"

"Oh, but I am. He thinks a really fantastic contemporary show can pull in a young adult audience. He virtually challenged me to prove *Goodbye, Again* is good enough to do it."

"And, of course, you fell right into his trap?"

"Trap? You mean did I agree to go along with him to get the series on the air? You're damn right I did," Barrie retorted heatedly. "I fought too long for this chance. I wasn't about to throw it away, just because the network pulled a stupid stunt like this. We can make the show work for eight o'clock."

"How?" Danielle sounded disgustingly pessimistic.

"By forgetting about the time slot and just doing a good television series. If it's funny at nine-thirty, it'll be just as funny at eight."

"Maybe on Wednesday, sweetie. Not on Saturday. On Saturday it had better be hysterical."

Barrie sighed. "So get Heath in here and start making it hysterical."

"That's your job. I'm only the director." Barrie glared at her, but before she could respond, the phone rang. When Barrie answered, she was greeted by the low, deep murmur of Michael's voice.

"Good morning, Barrie MacDonald." He sounded just as seductive this morning as he had on parting last night. Barrie's heart thundered loudly in her ears as she realized how easy it would be to become addicted to starting and ending her days like this.

"Good morning," she said calmly, unaware that her knuckles were turning white from clutching the receiver so tightly.

"Michael?" Danielle mouthed the name silently. At Barrie's nod, she grinned smugly, rose and tiptoed to the door. "I'll leave you alone," she whispered significantly as she waved cheerfully. Barrie had the oddest desire to strangle her.

"Barrie, are you there?"

"What?" she snapped, then softened her tone. "Yes, I'm here."

"Is everything okay?" He sounded genuinely concerned and somewhat puzzled.

"Everything's just fine, Mr. Compton. Why shouldn't it be?"

"You sound funny. And you're still calling me Mr. Compton. Are you upset about something?"

Barrie took a deep breath. "I am not upset... Michael," she protested tightly. "What do you want?"

"I want to see you."

"About what?" she asked cautiously.

He chuckled softly. "The usual," he taunted. "Do you always cross-examine a man who's asking you for a date?"

"I didn't realize that's what you had in mind," she said defensively. "We do have a business relationship, too, you know."

"Yes, I'm aware of that. It does tend to cloud the issue, doesn't it? Would you prefer it if I limited my professional calls to the workday and made my personal calls after hours?" he offered cheerfully.

Barrie promptly felt foolish and lightened her tone. "That assumes that both of us work predictable, normal hours. When was the last time you came in at nine and left at five?"

He paused for several seconds. "When I had the flu in 1977," he recalled at last. "I see your point. Where does that leave us?"

"I guess you'd better just state your business more clearly. For instance, you might suggest that we get together one evening for dinner and dancing. That is clearly a date," she explained.

"What if I ask you to go to a screening? Is that business or pleasure?"

"If you play your cards right, it could be both." Barrie heard the teasing comment as it came out of her mouth, and she cringed. She was asking for trouble, begging for it, in fact.

"Oh, really?" he said in a voice that suddenly lowered to a husky growl. "That sounds promising."

"Have any screenings lined up?" she taunted.

"Not for weeks."

"Too bad."

"How about dinner, then? I'll even cook."

"You're going to cook?" she retorted skeptically. "Is that the modern day equivalent of an invitation to view etchings?"

"Not in my case," he objected. "I take my skills as a chef seriously. I even have a food processor and a convection oven. So, how about it?"

"When?"

"Tonight."

Barrie gulped nervously. This was exactly the sort of contemporary fast-paced plunge-right-in courting she'd always believed in and had built into the concept for her series. No games, no promises, no commitment. Just dinner with a highly charged hint that passion was on the menu. So why did she want to shout that tonight was entirely too soon? Why did she have this persistent, nagging fear that men like this, men who swept you off your feet with a rush of attention, often dropped you in the dust just as quickly. It shouldn't matter one whit to her if Michael Compton walked into her life today and out tomorrow. In today's world you were supposed to shrug, say thanks for the memories and goodbye.

Barrie shivered. She'd gotten to be very good at goodbyes. Her father had taken off more frequently than the flights from Los Angeles International Airport. Each time Barrie had watched her mother's reserves of strength crumble a little more. She had sworn she would never be in that position and that no man would ever matter that much. She had built up defenses that would have made the combined forces of the army, navy and marines proud.

With all that practice at self-protection, she could have dinner again with Michael Compton, she decided resolutely. Tonight or next week. It wouldn't make any difference. She was perfectly capable of keeping her emotions in check.

"Tonight's just fine," she said firmly, then wondered at the little thrill of anticipation that rippled along her spine. It was not the response of a woman who was indifferent. It was another clear-as-a-bell warning signal, and she was paying absolutely no attention to it. She had to be crazy.

In a tone that was suddenly brisk and businesslike, indicating that he was probably no longer alone, Michael gave her his phone number and his address in Beverly Hills. "I'll see you about eight, then. Call if you get lost."

Barrie had barely hung up the phone when there was a knock on her door. "Yes?" A messenger entered.

"Miss MacDonald?" Barrie nodded. "I have a package for you."

When the messenger had deposited the huge, beautifully wrapped box on her desk and left, she took the card out of the envelope.

"Enjoy these and think of me, just as I'll be remembering last night. Michael."

She opened the box and found two pounds of huge ripe strawberries, which had been dipped in a rich dark chocolate. Her mouth immediately watered, and her pulse rate fluttered as she recalled Michael's obvious arousal as he watched her eat those strawberries at dinner. She took one from the box now and bit slowly into it, savoring the sweet taste of the berry and the bittersweet taste of the chocolate. She closed her eyes. It was absolutely heavenly. It was also a provocative indication that Michael was interested in more than her skills as a producer and was determined to tantalize her with reminders of his more personal intentions. He might be a hard-nosed broadcasting executive, but he obviously had the sweetly seductive soul of a romantic.

Before she could linger too long on the dangers of that combination, Danielle and Heath burst into the office in the midst of an already heated argument. Melinda Ashcroft, who'd been cast in the series's lead role, was right behind them, her hands on her hips, her mouth pursed in her distinctive, sexy pout.

"Barrie, I cannot ask Melinda to play this scene the way it's written," Danielle protested, throwing the open script down on Barrie's desk.

"It just doesn't feel right," Melinda agreed in the low, husky voice that could probably lure men to jump off cliffs. "Karen would not do something like that."

"What do you know about Karen?" Heath snarled. "I wrote this part, and I say she would do exactly that; she would storm into Mason's office and confront him."

"In the middle of a business conference?" Danielle said skeptically. "Come on, Heath. Karen is supposed to be a rational, understanding woman. She is not going to jeopardize a big deal for Mason by screeching at him like a banshee in front of total strangers."

Barrie listened carefully to the raging argument, glanced at the script and then finally decided she'd better intercede before Heath's blood pressure went through the roof again. Already the color in his neck was working its way from bright red to purple.

"Quiet!" she shouted to make herself heard over the uproar. Danielle, Heath and Melinda promptly fell silent and stared at her, obviously stunned by her emphatic, no-nonsense outburst. "That's better. Now would everyone please sit down, and let's discuss this like civilized adults."

The discussion lasted most of the morning, and much of it was far from civilized. Despite Barrie's best efforts to mediate, it seemed that her director, writer and the series's star were far too angry with one another to compromise. Finally she'd had about all of the bickering she intended to take.

"Okay, that's it," she announced decisively. "The scene stays. Karen wouldn't just sit back and suffer in silence."

Heath smirked triumphantly.

"However, Heath," she began, watching his smile fade. "I want you to tone it down slightly. Melinda and Dani are right. She might go barging into that office, but she would never blow up like that once she realized she was interrupting a business meeting. Maybe she'd pretend she came in for some other reason, or maybe she'd mutter something under her breath and leave. I don't know. You're the writer. Work on it. I want to see the new dialogue after lunch."

It was midafternoon before the rehearsal was back on track, and Barrie was determined to get one decent run-through before she let any of the cast off for the evening.

"Hon, I think we're wasting our time," Danielle told her at last. "Everybody's worn out. Why don't we call it quits and get on it again first thing in the morning?"

Barrie sighed and inquired wearily, "What time is it?"

"It's eight-fifteen."

"What? It can't be." She buried her head in her arms. "How could I do this?"

"Do what? What's wrong?"

"I was supposed to meet Michael for dinner fifteen minutes ago."

"And you forgot?" Danielle's voice was incredulous. "You had a date with the boss, and you've been sitting here worrying about props?"

"I haven't been worrying about props. I've been trying to keep you, Heath and Melinda from killing one another."

"Honey, don't you know that this was just a healthy disagreement among three rational adults?"

"Rational? Adults? You've got to be kidding. The three of you have been behaving like juvenile delinquents."

"That's just creative energy being unleashed," Danielle said airily.

"Well, why don't you use some of that creative energy to dream up an excuse I can give to Michael for being late?"

"How about the truth?"

"You want me to tell the vice president for pro-gramming of this network, who ultimately pays our salaries and decides whether we will be on the air longer than six weeks, you want me to tell him that I forgot about our date? Are you crazy?"

"I'm not the one who forgot the date with one of the most eligible bachelors in Los Angeles," Danielle reminded her smugly. "You did. You tell me who's crazy."

"I don't have time to stand here debating this with you. I'd better get myself over there before he burns whatever he's cooking. I have a feeling ruining his dinner would be an even bigger sin than forgetting it."

"You're going to his place? My, my!" The smug smirk was back.

"Don't say it, Dani, or I'll blame my delay on you. How do you suppose Michael would feel about that?"

"Okay. Okay. Get out of here," she replied with a laugh. "I'll send the cast home."

Barrie grabbed her purse and briefcase and headed for the door.

"See you in the morning," Danielle called out cheerfully, then added wickedly, "I can hardly wait to hear if those thighs are everything they seem to be."

"I do not intend to check out the man's legs," Bar-rie retorted indignantly.

"Right," she replied dryly. "You're only going over there to sample his favorite recipes."

"Exactly."

"Honey, the evening may start out with beef Stro-ganoff and asparagus vinaigrette, but I'll lay you odds that you're on the menu for dessert,'' she said with a wink.

"No way," Barrie insisted stoutly as she slipped out the door. But deep inside, where her stomach fluttered nervously and her blood sizzled, she wondered if she would have the strength to resist if Michael was really determined to have her.

Four

The drive from the studio into Beverly Hills, difficult under the best of conditions, had never seemed so long or the traffic so heavy. By the time Barrie was finally winding her way through the posh, unfamiliar neighborhood with its sculptured lawns and deceptively modest houses, it was already well after nine, pitch-dark, and virtually impossible for her to see the street signs clearly enough through those damned rose-tinted glasses to figure out where she was.

Terrific, she thought, as she peered vaguely through the windshield, then squinted at the address she'd scribbled down. Now she was completely lost in a tight-knit enclave not known for welcoming strangers. She was also just far enough from the nearest gas station or pay phone to make the idea of backtracking thoroughly unappealing. Assuming that she could even figure out how to backtrack. She sighed and tried to resign herself to the possibility of spending the rest of her life roaming the streets of Beverly Hills. Of course, she'd probably run out of gas or get picked up by the police long before that actually happened.

"Damn," she muttered in frustration as she pulled to the side of the palm-lined street and fumbled in the glove compartment for her map of L.A. Trying to hold the book so that she could read by the muted reflection of the streetlight, she finally found Michael's address. She glared at the map.

Of course his street was only one block long! She should have known he'd live somewhere so exclusive that it was barely on the map. However, it was only about a mile away and, barring any unexpected dead-ends—or restrictive gates—should be easy enough to reach if she just stayed straight about five blocks and turned left, then right, she decided at last.

As she crept along, squinting to read the street signs to locate the first turn, she murmured a silent prayer to the patron saint of lost souls to get her out of this fix, and quickly. Michael was going to be furious and, at this point, she wasn't any too thrilled about the situation herself. She hated being late almost as much as she abhorred being lost. The former made her feel guilty about her rudeness. The latter made her feel vulnerable, panicky in fact. And the combination was enough to send her fleeing home to burrow under the covers.

To top it off, she knew that this dinner had all sorts of hidden implications and dangers. Dangers best postponed for perhaps five or six years.

"I wonder if he'd believe that I developed a raging migraine that temporarily blocked out my memory and that I forgot all about dinner?" she asked herself aloud.

Not a chance, her conscience replied emphatically. He'd know you were being a coward.

It was probably fortunate, then, that before she could tell her conscience to go to blazes and then retreat to the security of her own bed, she found the street. After that it was an easy enough matter to find the address. There were only three houses on the whole blasted block.

It was nearly nine-thirty by the time she reluctantly walked up the palm-lined driveway and rang Michael's doorbell. When he opened the door, there was a worried frown on his face that altered into a tight, unwelcoming smile. Barrie shuddered. His mincemeat look was back.

"I've heard of being fashionably late, but don't you think this is overdoing it just a bit?" he asked.

The teasing question was light enough, but there was a hard edge to his voice that told Barrie he was really angry with her, far more angry than she'd anticipated he might be. Cautiously she put her hand on his arm.

"You really are upset with me, aren't you?" she said penitently. When he didn't respond, she rattled on nervously, "I don't blame you. I'm horribly late, but I was tied up at the studio working on the show longer than I expected. The traffic was awful. You know how that is this time of night. And then I got lost.'' She paused for breath and gazed at him hopefully. Nothing. Not even a blink of those blue-green eyes. She tried again. ''Anyway, I'm sorry. Did I ruin dinner?''

He stood looking down at her for a moment, then shook his head and smiled. This time it was more genuine. At least he didn't look as though he planned to kick her back out onto the streets anymore. ''Sorry. Of course not. I guess I was just afraid you'd changed your mind and decided to back out.''

One eyebrow arched quizzically. That did not sound like the brash, self-confident Michael Compton whom Barrie had seen so far. In fact, there was an appealing vulnerability to the comment that intrigued her. ''Are you serious?'' she asked, still not quite convinced she had actually heard that insecure note in his voice.

''Well, you were more than an hour late,'' he retorted more lightly. He grinned at her then, and the vulnerability vanished, replaced by a more familiar cockiness. ''Do you have any idea what it does to a man's ego to discover that an attractive woman is not nearly as anxious to see him as he is to see her?''

''I suspect your ego is doing just fine, Mr. Compton,'' Barrie replied sweetly. ''On the other hand, I have been battling trucks on the freeway, lost on the streets of Beverly Hills and starving to death in my Sentra, while you nibbled on...'' She looked at him impishly. ''On what? Carrot sticks?''

''Mushroom caps stuffed with crabmeat.''

Barrie sighed longingly as her mouth watered. She really was famished. She gazed boldly into his eyes and only barely resisted the urge to bat her long, dark lashes at him flirtatiously. "I don't suppose that if I apologized profusely for my tardiness I could talk you into sharing one or two of those with me?"

"That sounds like it might have some intriguing possibilities. Try it," he suggested, finally stepping aside to let her into the house. "I'm always open to an appeal from someone who's genuinely contrite."

"Don't press your luck, Mr. Compton," she flashed back. "Don't you know it's dangerous to tamper with a starving woman? You promised me dinner, and all I've gotten so far is static."

Those blue-green eyes of his roved possessively over her. "There is a certain amount of electricity in the air whenever we get together, isn't there?" he murmured softly as Barrie flushed under the intensity of his gaze and tried not to notice how well his jeans hugged those muscular thighs of his.

"That wasn't what I meant," she countered, but there was a decided lack of conviction in her voice.

"Maybe not," he said, gazing at her doubtfully, a definite twinkle in his eyes. "But it's true. Maybe we should explore the idea a bit after dinner."

Barrie returned his gaze boldly at first but finally blinked and looked away. Dessert, she thought as a nervous excitement rippled along her spine. It was exactly as Danielle had suspected. He thought she was on the menu for dessert. She swallowed and faced him again. Maybe if she kept her mind on the appetizers, she wouldn't feel quite so panicky about dessert. "What about those mushroom caps?"

He grinned at her knowingly. "Coming right up. Why don't you go on into the living room, and I'll be right with you. What would like to drink?"

"A glass of wine."

"Red or white?"

"White. Are you sure I can't help with something?"

"Nope. I've got everything under control."

I'll just bet you have, Barrie thought. Men like Michael Compton always did. As she waited, she explored the living room with its comfortably over-stuffed sofa and chairs in front of a blazing fire. The mantel and one wall were of a dark wood that gave the room a decidedly masculine feel. The darkness might have been oppressive, but the remaining walls had been papered with a light country French design, and French doors led out onto a brick patio that was softly lit by the moonlight. In the daytime those doors would let in plenty of sunlight, along with the sweet fragrance of the profusion of roses she could see blooming in every imaginable color from pale pink to bright red, from dazzling yellow to warm apricot. The bright turquoise of a free-form pool sparkled just beyond the edge of the terrace. It was simple and luxurious without being the least bit ostentatious, and Barrie had to admit that she was impressed by Michael's taste. His decor had a personal touch that she suspected was all his. She doubted that a decorator had been allowed near the place.

"Admiring the view?" his low, sensual voice whispered over her shoulder.

"It's lovely."

"I fell in love with it the minute I saw it. The previous owner had covered these incredible wood floors with some awful plush mauve carpet. He was also heavily into art deco with lots of pink and black. I practically had to close my eyes while I stripped the wallpaper."

"With your schedule, when did you find the time?"

"Late at night and on weekends. It took a while, but it was worth every minute. Besides, you have no idea how satisfying it is to rip up carpet and yank down wallpaper after a day of restraining every single urge to shred the imbeciles who parade through your office."

"If they're that bad, I'm surprised you bother to control yourself," she retorted dryly.

"I am, too, sometimes," he admitted. "But I know one thing about this business. The person who's trying to sell you some perfectly impossible concept that makes you want to scream one day may develop a unique, innovative series later that could be number one. If you've been rude, he may take that idea to another network. I'm not about to take that chance."

"So you suffer in silence."

He shook his head. "I prefer to think that I'm diplomatic. I'd also like to believe I can create an environment that encourages their creativity, instead of stifling it. If there's a shred of talent there, I want to nurture it."

As he talked, he almost absentmindedly played with a strand of Barrie's hair, tucking it behind her ear, his fingers soft and gentle against the side of her face. Barrie trembled at the touch, her body so responsive to his nearness that she knew she wouldn't have a prayer of refusing him anything he asked of her unless she backed out of his reach now. She sighed but didn't move. She couldn't.

In *Goodbye, Again*, with so much potential passion creating a crackling tension between the characters, there would be no hesitation tonight, no regrets tomorrow. But this wasn't a script, and suddenly Barrie realized Michael Compton was leaping over her well-established defenses in a single bound. The realization that he might actually begin to matter to her was terrifying.

"Hey," he said softly. "What is it?"

Barrie blinked and gazed into Michael's eyes. Had he read her mind, sensed the troubling thoughts? "Nothing," she lied. "Why?"

"You had this far away expression on your face for a minute there, and you seemed so sad." He shook his head. "No. That wasn't it. More scared, maybe. Vulnerable."

Startled by his perceptiveness, she forced a shaky smile and a brave, teasing tone. "You're imagining things. Were you reading one of those melodramatic soap opera scripts before I got here?"

He studied her closely, as though trying to decide whether to pursue the subject. To Barrie's relief, he apparently decided to let it drop. "Nope," he responded lightly. "I was slaving over a hot stove. Are you ready for dinner?"

"Absolutely. I've never known a man whose culinary skills went beyond cooking steaks on a backyard grill."

He regarded her indignantly. "My dear, I'll have you know that the French Chef is my favorite TV heroine."

"She's a little tall for you, isn't she?"

"Ah, but those recipes! *C'est magnifique!*" He gravely touched his fingers to his lips and blew a little kiss into the air.

Barrie chuckled. "If she affects you that strongly, I'm surprised you haven't put her back on the air in prime time."

"Believe me, I've thought about it. Can't you just imagine a whole situation comedy built around duck *à l'orange* and truffles?"

She appeared to consider the idea carefully. "Nope. Afraid not."

"Ah, Miss MacDonald, we must work on opening up your imagination."

He should only know, she thought dryly. Since meeting him just one short day ago, her imagination had been running wild, though admittedly the thoughts had very little to do with food or television. She'd had to fight to maintain her concentration during today's rehearsals for *Goodbye, Again*. Images of Michael had constantly popped into her mind. Images of the fire that blazed in his eyes when he looked at her. Even more disturbing images of the slim, athletic body, the rock-hard muscular thighs. In her mind, she had stripped him of his tailored jacket, his silk tie, his soft shirt and, finally, the slacks that hugged his hips and only barely camouflaged the strength of his legs. Her eyes had feasted on his masculinity, his potency, and she had trembled with a yearning so sharp that she'd thought for a moment the image was real.

And tonight it was. Or could be, if that was what she wanted. Michael was sitting across the table from her, and the shimmering candlelight paled in comparison to the bright flame of desire that burned in his eyes. Those unblinking eyes possessed her, cherished her, seduced her. Even as they dined on the delicious grilled salmon with dill sauce, his eyes told her his thoughts were elsewhere, in some special, intimate place where the two of them had become one.

Barrie's thoughts followed his, shared the intimacy, thrilled to the magic of his imagined touch. Unconsciously, she took a slow, provocative sip of wine, then ran her tongue over her dampened lips. Michael moaned and looked away, breaking the spell.

"Do you have any idea what you're doing to me, Barrie MacDonald?" he asked huskily.

If it was anything like what he was doing to her, she knew. But she also realized she had to deny it. To admit the truth would speed their relationship on a course from which there would be no retreat and that could only lead to disaster and pain.

"Barrie, I've told you before that I want us to be together," he said with straightforward honesty. "It was true last night. It's even more true tonight. You're an amazing woman. Intelligent, wise, funny, independent. The kind of woman I've always looked for but never found. And we're both mature adults. I understand your reservations, but we can handle this. We can keep our business and personal relationships separated."

It was a speech Heath Donaldson could have written, and it was spoken with absolute conviction, underlined with an undeniable urgency. If Barrie had read it in one of the scripts, heard it on the air, she would have believed it, would have thought desire and mutual respect were more than enough to justify a sexual relationship. The Karen Devereaux she had created for *Goodbye, Again*, had been patterned on her own liberated beliefs. So, she thought, why wasn't the sort of quick and easy intimacy Michael was suggesting enough for her tonight? Why was there this sudden empty feeling in the pit of her stomach?

The answer to that was easy and disturbing. She and Michael would be good together. Too good. A warm ache deep inside told her that with unerring, sizzling accuracy. But, for the first time in her life, she had a feeling it would not be nearly enough and that with Michael she would want much more, perhaps something that could never be.

Don't forget your promise, she reminded herself sharply. She had sworn all her life that she would never be as vulnerable as her mother had been. There would be no painful goodbyes for her, only breezy farewells. And to accomplish that, no one could ever get too close, especially not someone like Michael with whom intimacy would almost inevitably lead to emotional involvement.

To top it off, Michael held far too much potential power over her. Not only could he chop her heart into little pieces, he could control, even destroy, her professional future. The risks were tremendous.

Barrie shook her head. "Not a good idea," she said firmly, amazed at the strength in her voice, when she was so shaky and unsure inside. "In fact, I think I'd better be leaving."

"Running away?" he taunted.

"Of course not." She was merely retreating to get her line of defenses back into place. There was a difference, but she doubted if Michael would see it. She wasn't sure if she could explain it to him, either, so she didn't even try.

"Do you have work to do, then?"

"No."

"Then stay a little longer." His eyes pleaded with her. His words were softly, persuasively spoken. "Go for a walk with me."

She sensed his acceptance of her retreat and appreciated it, though she remained skeptical. "A walk?"

His eyes twinkled at her doubtful tone. "You remember walking. It's one of those quaint old customs that people used to indulge in before the advent of the automobile. It's very useful in getting from one location to another."

"Sounds intriguing. Did you have a particular destination in mind?"

"Nope. That's the wonderful part of walking. You just start out and go wherever your impulses take you."

Barrie regarded him cautiously. The suggestion seemed innocent enough, and surely his impulses wouldn't lead her into some sort of romantic trap in the middle of Beverly Hills. And it was a lovely night. The dry heat of midafternoon had given way to a cool, teasing breeze. The clear midnight black of the sky was dusted with silvery sparkles, and a full moon hung low over the mountains.

"Okay," she agreed finally. "Let's walk."

"Do you have a jacket with you?"

"No."

"Then I'll loan you one of mine." He pulled a bright blue windbreaker from the closet and draped it around her shoulders.

Barrie hugged the jacket to her and inhaled the intoxicating, woodsy aroma of his after-shave that lingered in the material. She felt almost as though she were wrapped in his arms, snug and protected. It was a dangerously pleasant feeling, an addictive feeling.

Prepared to walk briskly along, Barrie was surprised to find that Michael's pace was leisurely, and he'd meant what he said about exploring. As they passed each house, he told her brief, insightful anecdotes about his neighbors. Within minutes she had a clear image of the aging movie queen who never went out to pick up her morning paper without first dressing up and putting on her makeup, of the real estate tycoon whose legendary deals regularly made the business pages of the newspaper, of the couple whose regular marital spats—and subsequent reunions—were both colorful and noisy.

"And what do they say about you?" she teased. "I can just hear them, 'Oh, that Michael Compton is something else. Wild parties every week. A steady stream of starlets parading to the door. Why, goodness me, I don't know how the poor man does it. He must take megadoses of vitamins.'"

"Actually, I think they've been horribly disappointed. Not one single starlet has entered my front door, and our dinner tonight is the closest I've come to throwing a party."

"I don't believe it," she scoffed. "One of the most powerful men in television, and you paint a sad little scenario of a lonely, isolated existence."

"Hey, who said anything about lonely? I'm a very self-contained person. I don't need to be surrounded by people to have a good time. I don't need to have my ego stroked regularly just to keep functioning. In this business you can have a whole mob of acquaintances around anytime you want them, but I choose my friends carefully. They're people who genuinely like me for who I am, not because of the job I hold."

How ironic, Barrie thought, listening to Michael's thoughtful explanation of his chosen life-style. He was right. So many people would have given anything to be drawn into Michael Compton's inner circle simply because of his position at the network. Other producers—male and female—would have envied this closeness she was sharing with him, this apparent opportunity to further her career. Yet it was precisely because of his network position that she was having so much difficulty accepting him as a friend, much less a lover.

Suddenly he was tugging on her hand, like a child urging a parent on to sample the possibilities of some wonderful new adventure that had caught his eye. "Over here," he said, his eyes glittering with pure excitement.

"Where?" she asked. "All I see is a playground."

"Exactly. When was the last time you played on swings?"

"When I was much younger," she said dryly. "In fact, well before puberty set in."

"Then it's about time you tried it again. You're getting jaded. You probably get your thrills from fancy roller coasters and flashy video games. You can't beat the simple pleasure of flying high into the darkness, trying to touch the stars."

Barrie looked at him curiously. What an amazing blend of seemingly contradictory traits had been packaged into Michael Compton's gorgeous body! A boy's excitement in innocent pleasures and the strong physical desires of a grown man. The self-assured strength of a natural leader and the gentleness of a lover. The quick, sometimes cynical mind of a hardened realist and the quiet, introspective soul of a romantic.

"Come on," he urged her. "Hop up. I'll push you to get you started. Ready?"

Barrie nodded and felt his hands firm and possessive on her waist, pulling her back until her body was against his. Just when she felt her nerves come alive with an unbearable tension, he released her, sending her flying forward. The climb high into the sky was exhilarating. The descent into his waiting hands was even more thrilling. With each release, she swung higher and higher until she was laughing at the sheer joy of the feeling, exulting in the rush of air against her cheeks, the breeze rippling through her hair.

"Having fun?"

"It's wonderful," she admitted, the words flying away on the whoosh of wind created by her arc through the sky. "I feel free, exactly the way a bird must feel when it soars away from the earth. Why aren't you doing it?"

"I'd rather watch you," he said, moving around to stand in front of her, just beyond her reach as her legs pumped to keep up the motion he had created for her. "You look like a little girl, all rosy-cheeked and happy."

Barrie caught an odd wistfulness in his voice. "Is there something wrong?"

He shook his head. "Not really."

"Not really means there is. You just don't want to talk about it."

"I just don't want to spoil the moment."

"Is what you were thinking about that serious?"

"Not serious exactly. I just wish you could relax with me the way you have out here."

"But I am with you."

"It's not the same, Barrie MacDonald, and you know it. I have the feeling you're afraid of me or of yourself. You're afraid to let yourself go with me, just the way you were before you climbed on that swing. But you did that. You took that risk. Why can't you take one with us?"

He stepped closer and caught her as the swing came forward, holding the edge of the seat, his fingers nestled so innocently against her thighs that she couldn't complain, yet so provocatively close that it was impossible for her to ignore them.

"Are you afraid of losing control? Is that it?" he asked gently. "Because I'm not trying to destroy your independence, you know. I don't expect you to yield to me because I'm a man and you're a woman. We're equals, Barrie. I respect your creativity, your intelligence, your spunk. Why would I want to change any of that, to make you less than you can be?"

Barrie sighed heavily. "You might not mean to, but that's what would happen," she said, her voice filled with years of pent-up bitterness. "I've seen it before. Two people get involved with the best intentions in the world, and pretty soon one of them is doing all of the giving, making all of the compromises. Usually it's the woman because men have no idea how to go about making concessions. It's *their* career that's important, *their* needs that must be met."

Her eyes flashed at him, filled with fire and challenge. "That's not for me. I've worked hard to get where I am, and no one is going to take it away."

Michael was shaking his head, and there was something in his eyes that she couldn't quite read. Understanding, maybe. Compassion. "I would never try," he said simply.

"You can't say that. You of all people. Not only could you ask it of me as a man, but you could demand it as my boss. Is it any wonder I'm terrified of getting closer to you?"

He sighed, and a great sorrow seemed to fill his eyes. He didn't even pretend not to understand. "No. It's no wonder. I guess it's just going to take more time for me to prove to you that you have nothing to fear from me."

"Michael, don't even say that. You know that if you want to, you can and will order changes in my show. If it comes to that, you'll even cancel it. Don't tell me I have nothing to be afraid of. I have more to fear from you than any other man on earth."

Before he could say another word, she ran. Ran until her lungs were filled to bursting and her side ached. Then she walked the remaining blocks back to his house and got into her car. Her head was spinning with the words she had just hurled at him and with the terrifying awareness of their accuracy. She did fear Michael Compton's power. But more than that, she feared his sensuality and the damnable combination of wit, attractiveness and intelligence that lured her, taunted her body and mind in ways she'd never dreamed possible. She had a feeling there was more danger in that pull than she could even begin to imagine.

Five

The next day seemed to prove her point, demonstrating in graphic detail why any personal relationship with Michael would be sheer folly, why it could seriously jeopardize her career and play havoc with not only her emotions, but the very values—her values—that were at the core of *Goodbye, Again*. Barrie was sitting on the set going over the revised script for the opening episode with Danielle, when Kevin Porterfield came running in, his expression harried, his eyes shining with self-importance.

"Miss MacDonald, I have a memo for you from Mr. Compton. It's urgent," he announced breathlessly as he skidded to a halt in front of them. In his jeans, oxford cloth shirt and hand-knit sweater, he looked exactly like what he was: A very recent graduate of an Ivy League university film program.

Barrie tried not to show her irritation at the interruption. Ever since Kevin had been assigned to the show as network liaison, she'd had to remind herself she had once been his age and just as eager. She only prayed she hadn't been quite so pompous.

"I'm sure it is, Kevin. Put it on my desk. I'll look at it later."

"But you have to look at it now. It's about the first episode."

Barrie peered at him over the top of her glasses. "What about the first episode?" There was a dangerous edge in her voice.

Kevin avoided her gaze. He'd apparently detected the note of barely restrained antagonism and decided that any further involvement with the message might not be in his own best interests. "I don't know," he denied feebly.

Barrie didn't believe him for a minute. "Of course you do. I'm sure you read the memo on the way over here. Oh, never mind. Hand it over."

Her eyes skimmed over the terse, impersonal note, which was scrawled across a speed memo form: "Scene 3 in act 2 is entirely too suggestive for an eight o'clock show. Clean it up or take it out."

When she'd finished reading it, Barrie calmly shredded the memo into tiny pieces and spilled them onto the floor. "Okay, Danielle, let's get on with it."

Danielle eyed her warily. "That's all? That's all you're going to say? What did he want you to do?"

"It doesn't matter. I'm not doing it."

"But, Miss MacDonald . . ." Kevin began, a hint of desperation in his voice. He was apparently seeing his career go up in the smoke of Michael Compton's fiery outrage.

"Kevin, I am not changing one word of this show. Go tell that to your boss."

"But . . . but," he sputtered helplessly.

"You can't make poor Kevin do your dirty work for you," Danielle chided her.

"Why not? Michael sent him over here to do his."

"Ahhh. I see. That's the real problem, isn't it? You're mad because he didn't come over here himself."

Barrie glowered at her. "Correction. I am furious because he is trying to tamper with the integrity of my series. I don't give a hang who delivers the message."

"Right," Danielle said skeptically.

"Okay, so maybe that does tick me off," she admitted reluctantly. "But the point is that I have no intention of following his orders when they make absolutely no sense for the show. It's not my fault he put an adult sitcom in a kiddie time slot."

"Don't you think you ought to be the one to go tell him that? Work out some sort of compromise?"

Barrie looked at Danielle as though she'd grown two heads. "Do you actually think I should compromise on this?" she asked incredulously.

"I think you should at least listen to what the man has to say. Maybe he had a point."

Barrie's sigh teetered between disgust and resignation. Ever since college where they'd been roommates, Danielle had always appealed to the more rational side of her mind. Sometimes she hated Dani for it.

"All right," she grumbled. "I'll go over there." She stared at Danielle defiantly. "But I am not budging on this. He put the show on at eight o'clock. He's going to have to live with the consequences."

"No, sweetie pie. We are."

Barrie threw up her hands and stormed out of the studio, mumbling angrily to herself all the way across the parking lot to the executive offices. By the time she reached Michael's suite, she had worked up a full head of steam and formulated a diatribe that would make Michael's apparently overly sensitive ears burn. Too suggestive, indeed!

Marching past a startled Mrs. Hastings, Barrie ignored the secretary's frantic effort to restrain her and slammed into the inner office.

"Okay, Michael," she snapped, her brown eyes flashing sparks. "What's the meaning of this... this..."

Her outburst sputtered to a halt as she realized that she was staring into several astonished faces. "Oh, my..."

"I'm sorry, Mr. Compton," Mrs. Hastings apologized hastily from behind her. "I tried to stop her."

"That's true. She did. I just didn't listen. I didn't know," she muttered in embarrassment, wondering how the devil Heath had gotten Karen out of this situation in the script. If it hadn't been for Michael's ill-timed memo, she would have had a chance to read those new pages of dialogue and would have the words she needed to get out of this room gracefully. No, forget graceful. It was far too late. She just needed something to get her out of this room and into some kind of deep, dark hole.

Since words—hers and Heath's—escaped her, she merely backed toward the door, noting that Michael, the louse, seemed to be finding the situation incredibly amusing. At least he was grinning. She had a feeling, though, that there might not be a lot of humor behind that tight smile.

"Wait, Miss MacDonald," he said softly, though there was no mistaking the command in his voice. "Did you want something?"

Torn between embarrassment and still-seething anger, she shook her head mutely.

"You must have wanted something, Miss Mac-Donald," he repeated patiently. "I'm sure we'd all like to hear it."

Several faces watched her expectantly. She had to admit Michael was a master. He'd taken this lousy rotten moment and turned it to his complete advantage. "Later," she ground out between clenched teeth. "We can discuss it later."

"Why don't you wait outside, then? We'll be through here in just a minute." She heard the steely tone beneath the innocuous words. It was an order, no doubt about it.

Although the embarrassing incident had tempered her fury quite a bit, Barrie sat in the outer office and tried to nurse it back to health. It would never do to walk into Michael's office like some whimpering child, just because she had happened to make an absolute fool of herself.

"Would you like some coffee while you wait?" Mrs. Hastings asked kindly.

"No, thank you." With the state her nerves were in already, if she drank any more caffeine, she'd come completely unglued. She noted Mrs. Hastings's sympathetic expression and asked, "How furious is he really?"

"Well, it is an important meeting with some major advertisers," she began as Barrie moaned and hid her face. "But I wouldn't worry too much about it, dear."

"How can you say that? You said it was important."

"Yes, but you didn't let me finish," she said, her eyes twinkling. "Mr. Compton absolutely hates meeting with advertisers. I'm sure you provided a very welcome distraction."

"Right," Barrie said skeptically. "One of his producers comes barging in like a madwoman, and it absolutely thrills him to pieces. I'm sure it will do wonders for sales, too."

"Think of it this way, dear. It will break up the meeting early," she offered. Then, lowering her voice, she added with a conspiratorial smile, "I wasn't supposed to call in with a fake crisis for another half hour."

Barrie's eyebrows rose disbelievingly. So much for her desire to imbue Mrs. Hastings with saintly honesty. She was obviously, first and foremost, a loyal secretary. Barrie's lips twitched. "You were actually going to do that?"

Mrs. Hastings shrugged, but her blue eyes twinkled merrily. "I told you he hates meeting with advertisers."

Just then the door swung open, and the three men in their identical gray pin-striped suits were ushered out the door by a beaming Michael. Even without Mrs. Hastings's comments, Barrie would have known the heartiness toward them was feigned. As soon as they were out the door, his mouth settled into a grim line, and he faced Barrie. She thought she saw his lips twitching, but perhaps that had only been wishful thinking. His words were certainly curt enough.

"Now, Miss MacDonald, shall we try your entrance again? This time with a little less flamboyance."

Inside, he shut the door firmly behind them. Barrie had the oddest desire to ask that it be left open, so that Mrs. Hastings could be a witness when he decided to wring her neck. He walked back to his desk and sat down on the edge, waving her to a chair.

"I'd rather stand," she said stiffly.

"As you like. What's the problem?"

"I'm sure you know exactly what the problem is. I received your memo, which you didn't even have the decency to deliver yourself."

Blue-green eyes as hard as glass bored into her. Barrie winced. This was even worse than she'd expected. There was no warmth in those eyes, not even a flicker of the heat that had caressed her last night before she ran out on him. It was as though she were talking to a stranger.

Or to a boss, she reminded herself sternly. When was she going to learn to be more diplomatic? She sighed and thought probably never. She would always stand up for what she believed in, would always be thoroughly outspoken, and damn the consequences. The consequences right now did not seem to bode well for her future relationship—business or otherwise—with Michael Compton.

"I do not deliver memos," he informed her pointedly. "I write them."

Inwardly Barrie winced. Of course he did. They might have a personal relationship, but that certainly shouldn't imply that he should give her preferential treatment. She wouldn't even want him to. She sounded like a spoiled, petulant child.

"Okay, forget that. I don't suppose it really matters who delivers the memos around here," she conceded grudgingly. "The point is that I cannot do an adult situation comedy if you persist in tearing the guts out of the show."

For five minutes, as Michael calmly watched without a single change of expression, she paced around the office and argued passionately in defense of the scene he'd ordered cut. When she'd finally wound down, he said succinctly, "The scene goes."

Stunned by the finality of the comment, Barrie just stood and stared. "Didn't you hear a word I said?"

"Every one of them."

"And you're still determined to do this?"

"Yes."

"Then I don't know what you want from me," she said at last. "I don't know how you expect me to do this show."

"Tastefully, Miss MacDonald. I expect you to do it tastefully. You're trying too hard for sexy sophistication. There's too much glib chatter and cynical 'live it up in the fast lane' behavior. The audience will never buy it. They won't identify with it. Real people with deeply ingrained values don't act that way. That's as much of a fantasy as *Father Knows Best*. And you, of all people, should know it."

Barrie regarded him indignantly, her brown eyes flashing. "What do you mean?"

"You walked out on me last night, when you wanted to stay, didn't you?" Michael's eyes met hers, captured them, held them in a passionate duel.

"Who says I wanted to stay?" she fired back, the show momentarily forgotten.

"I do," he said softly, taking the few steps necessary to close the gap between them. His fingers trailed along her cheek, curved to cup her chin and remained there as his mouth descended slowly toward hers. Barrie's whole body tensed at the touch, fought against the feelings that were sweeping through her, proving his point. When his lips brushed across hers, the tender caress was like the offer of a blazing fire to someone who's been chilled by the night air. She moved irrevocably toward it, sought its comforting warmth. Her arms hung by her sides, her fingers curled into tight, angry fists. In her mind she saw herself pulling away, slapping his face, shouting at him that he was wrong. But deep inside, where that gentle kiss had set a wildfire blazing, she knew that it was a lie, knew beyond a doubt that she did want him, had wanted to stay with him last night, had left only to protect...what? Her lifelong vision of an unencumbered carefree future?

At last she forced herself to listen to her head, to the cries of danger, and moved away from him.

There was a glimmer of amusement in his eyes, a taunting satisfaction as she slipped out of his grasp. "I rest my case," he said softly.

"Oh, go to blazes," she snapped. "So what have you proved? That I'm attracted to you? Big deal. There's no accounting for the whims of hormones. What does that have to do with this scene? Last night...right now, that was about you and I, not Mason and Karen."

Michael smiled at her gently. "I'd say the similarity is pretty striking."

"Michael, this show is not about you and me. It's fiction. And I think the story needs this scene to move forward."

"I think we need that scene to move forward, too," he taunted. "But you don't pay any attention to me. Why should Mason have better luck than I do?"

Barrie stared at him incredulously. "That is the most peculiar bit of logic in support of censorship that I've ever heard."

"How about I'm the boss and what I say goes?"

"And what I believe doesn't matter?"

Suddenly Michael's lips formed a thin, very determined line. "Not in this case. No. I'm sorry."

"I see."

Without another word, Barrie turned and left the office, refusing to let him see the tears that glittered in her dark brown eyes. Her heart felt as though Michael had tap-danced across it. She'd had creative disagreements before. In fact, she had lost many of them. She should have been used to it. So why did this one hurt so much?

Because it had been so personal, because Michael had taken that scene and linked it to their relationship. He, too, had apparently recognized that she was Karen. That recognition made his criticism hurt all the more. It was as though he were judging her, saying that her sense of morality was wrong. But it was the way most liberated women felt today, wasn't it? She wrestled with that question all the way back to the studio.

The short walk had never seemed to take quite so long. Nor had it ever been quite so lonely.

Six

_____

Barrie slowly pushed open the heavy door to the studio and went inside. She had never before felt so thoroughly and utterly defeated. The sight of Danielle, Heath and Kevin, seated in a tense, silent circle, didn't help. They were studying her expectantly, anxiously awaiting word of the outcome of her meeting. She knew that Danielle and Heath, at least, expected a victory.

"Well?" Danielle asked.

"The scene goes," she said tersely and marched into her office. Danielle immediately rose and followed.

"Want to talk about it?" she asked, closing the door.

"About what? We lost. End of report."

"Not about that. About whatever it is that has you looking as though you've lost your best friend."

Barrie looked at her oddly. "Is that how I look?"

"Exactly."

"Funny," she said, and there was a note of sadness in her voice. "That's how I feel, too."

Danielle studied her for several minutes. "You're not just upset because Michael insisted on the change, are you?"

"What makes you say that?"

"Because I know you. You're stubborn, and you stand up for what you believe in, but you usually concede defeat more gracefully than this."

"Okay. You're right," she admitted reluctantly. "There is more to it. Good heavens, Dani, I've worked on enough shows now to know that there will be changes. It comes with the territory."

"But those weren't your shows," Danielle reminded her. "Maybe your pride is on the line here."

"True, and that's part of it, I suppose. I love *Goodbye, Again* with my whole heart. I believe in it. But there's more to it than that."

Danielle appeared puzzled. "What more could there be?"

Barrie sank down wearily in the chair behind her desk. When she spoke at last, her voice was filled with frustration and pain. "Dani, he didn't even listen to me. I walked in there to try to discuss this rationally..."

"Rationally?" Danielle repeated skeptically.

Barrie grinned. "Okay, so I came on like an outraged fishmonger's wife. But I knew what I was talking about. I had perfectly valid arguments, and he paid absolutely no attention to them. He'd already made up his mind.''

"Network programmers aren't known for their open-mindedness. That shouldn't come as a big surprise to you, either, and at least you tried.''

"But this is Michael,'' she said plaintively.

Danielle's blond eyebrows arched quizzically over gray eyes that were filled with sudden understanding. "And you're falling in love with him.''

Barrie stared at her, openmouthed. "No! Never!'' she snapped indignantly. "Don't be ridiculous. I hardly know the man.''

"You know that he's strong, intelligent, funny, powerful and has terrific legs. If you ask me, he's what you've been looking for all your life. He may be the one man in the world who won't let you trounce all over him. Are you sure that isn't what this is all about? A last minute flurry of defiance before you take a tumble straight into his arms?''

"Danielle, for a woman who professes to be my friend, you have a very odd way of being supportive.''

"I'm only trying to make you see the obvious.''

"That I've fallen for Michael Compton?''

"Uh-huh,'' she said with a smirk. "Like the proverbial ton of bricks.''

"You're crazy.''

"If that's not it, then why does one little disagreement over the content of this show matter so much?'' she asked smugly.

"Because it's as though he's rejecting me, my beliefs, my values. You'd hate it, too, if someone tried to make mincemeat out of your convictions."

"Of course I would," Danielle agreed readily enough. Too readily. Barrie waited for the kicker. Danielle grinned. "Especially if I happened to be in love with him and wanted his approval more than anything."

"I repeat," she said stoutly, "I am not in love with Michael Compton."

"Right," Danielle said dryly. "And I'm the world's skydiving champion." She winked as she staged a perfectly executed tactical retreat. Her directorial sense of timing had never been better.

"See you on the set," she murmured as she closed the door with an emphatic click.

Barrie watched her leave, then shuffled the papers on her desk as she tried to figure out just why she felt so miserable. She refused to concede the possibility that Danielle might be right and that she could be falling in love with Michael Compton. That was too absurd to consider. True, he was all of those things Danielle had said, and more. He was sensitive and kind, and he challenged her in ways no other man ever had. He had even told her he wanted her to be the very best she could be. Not that she'd believed him. That was a line many men used, right before they asked you to give up something important. Good Lord, just look at what he'd asked her to do today.

Worse, his rejection of her arguments, his refusal to even really consider them, had seemed so arbitrary. That hurt even more coming from a man who permitted all sorts of violence and mayhem, to say nothing of some of the steamiest sex on television, after nine o'clock at night. On the other hand, she wasn't being permitted even the tiniest indiscretion, just because it would occur at 8:21. Where was the logic in that?

Not that arguing the point with him would do a bit of good. He had been pretty adamant, and she'd seen enough of his stubborn streak in the past couple of days to know it was a lost cause. They would just have to figure out some way to make the episode work without tearing the heart out of the show. Heath could do it, if he had to. He wouldn't sell out the show's integrity in the process, either.

But before she could think of a single tip to give him to help him pull off that bit of magic, someone tapped on her door.

"Yes."

The door opened, and Michael peered in hesitantly, as though expecting a barrage of well-aimed missiles to greet him. "Still mad?"

Barrie glowered at him, though her blasted traitorous heart flipped over happily. She managed to keep an edge in her voice. "Furious. What are you doing here?"

"I thought maybe you'd like to go out with me tonight and forget about all of this."

Barrie shook her head in amazement. "You really are something. How do you manage to keep your personal life and your professional life in such tidy little separate compartments?"

"Practice," he informed her smugly. "Come out with me, and I'll give you some tips."

"Forget it. I have a script to revise, or have you forgotten?"

"Hardly. But you also have a perfectly competent writer to do it for you."

"We work as a team around here."

"Can't one member of the team take the night off?" he asked, perching on the edge of her desk and pulling two tickets out of his pocket. He waved them at her. "Box seats for the Dodgers against the Reds. It could decide who gets in the play-offs."

"A baseball game?" she asked incredulously. Was the man psychic? How had he known that it was the one thing that might tempt her? She could have refused the symphony, a play, or even a very romantic moonlit sailboat ride to Catalina. She could not resist baseball.

She eyed him warily. "How did you know?"

He grinned at her and, despite her best effort at resistance, her blood sizzled. "That you like baseball? I make it a point to get to know everything I can about my people."

"Danielle and her big mouth," Barrie muttered under her breath. Aloud she said only, "Okay, Compton. What time?"

"I'll pick you up at six. We'll have dinner at the stadium."

"The man who whips up gourmet meals in a flash is going to condescend to eat hot dogs?"

His eyes flashed, dazzling her with their amused glitter. "Peanuts and popcorn, too."

"What! No crackerjacks?"

"Be nice to me, and I'll get some for you," he taunted.

"I am never that nice," she replied haughtily.

"So I've noticed. See you at six."

"Don't you need my address?"

"I've got it," he said smugly. "Haven't you caught on yet? I know just about everything about you. For instance, there's this cute little birthmark..."

Her mouth dropped open. "Why you..."

His deep laugh rumbled through the office. "Careful, Miss MacDonald."

Barrie picked up her Rolodex and started to throw it at him but decided she was in no mood to pick up all those little cards if the thing flew apart. Besides, tonight would be soon enough to get even with him. He might have learned about her passion for baseball, but she doubted if he'd also discovered that her loyalties were with *her* home team, the Cincinnati Reds. She wondered if that mile-wide macho protective streak of his extended to saving one very vocal Cincinnati fan from the wrath of an entire Dodger crowd.

She grinned impishly. It was going to be a very interesting evening, and whatever happened was going to serve him right. As for that birthmark, she thought stoutly, hell could freeze over before he'd get to see that firsthand.

When Michael arrived promptly at six to pick her up, he didn't seem to attach any special significance to the fact that she was wearing a red-and-white pinstriped blouse with a pair of bright red walking shorts. He seemed much more interested in her slender bare legs, and for a fleeting instant she wondered if the shorts had been a bad idea. Nope, not in this heat, she decided firmly, ignoring his all-too-appreciative gaze.

They made the drive to Dodger Stadium in record time and were in their seats well before the first pitch was thrown. As soon as they were sitting down, Barrie reached into her purse and extracted a large button proclaiming her a member of the Rose Garden. As she pinned it on her collar, Michael looked from the button to her perfectly bland expression and back again.

"Pete Rose?" he asked weakly.

"Of course," she responded casually as she reached back into her purse and pulled out a red-and-white Cincinnati banner. He seemed to turn pale beneath his perfect California tan.

"Why didn't you tell me?" he asked in a choked voice.

She beamed at him. "I thought you already knew everything about me."

"You think you're a real wise guy, don't you? You knew I had no idea you were a Reds fan."

"Does it matter?" she asked innocently. "I don't mind if you want to cheer for the Dodgers. Of course, it will be a losing cause."

"Like hell," he grumbled, getting to his feet. "I'll be right back."

"Bring me a hot dog, would you?"

He gave her a curt nod as he stalked off through the stands. Barrie chuckled as she watched him go. This was wonderful, even better than she'd anticipated. Michael clearly took his baseball very seriously. As she did.

While he was away, she read through the program and watched the players warm up on the field. Seeing the Reds in action again was like going back to her childhood, when she and her father had made the drive to Cincinnati's Riverfront Stadium on his infrequent visits home. Those baseball games had been the only times they had connected, the only times when he'd even seemed to notice she was alive. Ever since she'd been in L.A., she had made it a point to go to see the Reds play at least once when they came to town. It always brought back one of the few good memories she had of her father, though try as she might, it couldn't temper the bitterness.

"Here's your hot dog." Michael's gruff words interrupted her reveries. When she looked up, she almost burst out laughing. He was wearing a blue Dodger cap and had the stick holding a Dodger pennant tucked in his belt to free his hands for the cardboard tray of hot dogs and beers.

"I see you're getting into the spirit of this," she taunted lightly.

"You bet I am. Maybe we should make a little wager on the outcome of this game, just to make it interesting," he suggested with a wickedly seductive little glimmer in his eyes.

Barrie licked her lips nervously. "Umm...I think it will be plenty interesting without that."

"Coward." There was a definite challenge in Michael's quietly spoken taunt, and there was no way Barrie was going to ignore it. She was too much of a scrapper.

"Okay, Compton. What's the bet?"

"If Cincinnati wins, I will take you to that benefit gala at the Dorothy Chandler Pavilion next week." He gazed at her significantly. "And if the Dodgers win, you'll come home with me tonight."

She shook her head adamantly. "Nice try, but that's no bet. You win either way."

He brushed a finger across her lips to silence her doubts. "So do you," he promised softly, setting off a series of tiny flutters in Barrie's abdomen. She opened her mouth to speak, but no words would come out. She licked her lips and tried again.

"How about letting me do the show the way I want to, if Cincinnati wins. That's a real bet."

He shook his head. "Sorry. No deal. I don't play games with my professional decisions."

Barrie sighed. "It was worth a try."

"How about my terms? Will you accept them?"

She glanced out on the field as if in search of reassurance that the Reds would not let her down and get her in even deeper with Michael before the night was out. Did she dare to accept a bet that might land her in his bed? Suddenly she grinned to herself. The bet said nothing about where she would sleep tonight. A loss by Cincinnati only dictated where they would go after the game. Even though Michael might have a very clear impression of what he wanted to happen when they got there, she was still perfectly capable of saying no.

Or yes.

She gave him a dazzling smile. "It's a deal," she agreed.

For the next three hours the battle lines between them had been drawn. Whenever Michael cheered for the Dodgers, Barrie glared at him. When she screamed for the Reds, he glowered back. On a particularly close call, they nearly came to blows.

"He was out by a mile," Michael shouted victoriously.

"Are you kidding?" Barrie grumbled. "You're as blind as the umpire. My man was lying across the base, while your guy was still fumbling around in the dirt for the ball."

"The umpire was right on it. He called him out."

"He needs bifocals."

"You're just a sore loser."

"I haven't lost yet, Compton. The score's tied."

"And the Dodgers are coming to bat."

"Big deal. It's the bottom of the batting order."

"They'll send in a pinch hitter for the pitcher."

"Who made you the manager?"

"It's the only thing that makes sense, especially in the bottom of the ninth."

The first batter walked.

"So what?" Barrie muttered at Michael's triumphant expression.

"I didn't say a word."

The second batter hit a sharp single down the right field line, sending the runner racing around second and into third base. Michael was on his feet, yelling his head off. Barrie was biting her nails.

"I am not going to get discouraged," she muttered under her breath. The game was not over yet.

"Come on, damn it, strike him out!" she shouted at the top of her lungs, her face flushed with excitement. The pitcher complied. "Way to go! Two more! You can do it."

She ignored the fiery disapproval in Michael's eyes and the glares of the fans around them. "Come on, baby. You can do it," she repeated defiantly. The next player struck out.

"Okay. You've done the worst of it. Only one more."

Michael was back in his seat, and now she was on her feet. "Strike him out," she urged.

The bat met the ball with a sharp crack that sent a shiver of fear tripping along her spine. She watched as the ball sailed high into center field. "It's an easy catch," she murmured softly. "Get it. Get it." The ball plopped into the centerfielder's glove, and she waved her banner triumphantly.

When she glanced down into Michael's face, she noted the unexpected amusement in his eyes. "What's so funny?" she asked curiously.

"You. I have never seen anyone who professes to such sophistication get quite so carried away at a baseball game."

She grinned back at him. "You've been doing a fair amount of shouting yourself."

He nodded sheepishly, as if surprised by the discovery. "That's true. I think you must bring out my competitive spirit."

"Either that, or you just want to win your bet."

He grinned at her. "There is that," he agreed. "We could call it off," he offered generously.

"Not on your life. I feel a victory coming on."

Cincinnati scored twice in the top of the tenth to Barrie's absolute delight and Michael's dismay. The Dodgers managed to put three men on base in the bottom of the inning before a relief pitcher came in and struck out the next three batters to end the game.

"So," she said, still waving her banner in triumph. "What night is that gala?"

"We'll discuss it later," Michael groused as they made their way to the car.

"Don't be a sore loser," she taunted him. "Even if I'd come home with you, you wouldn't have gotten to first base."

"No pun intended?"

"Sorry. No."

"Are you so sure?" he wondered, studying her thoughtfully as they stood beside the car.

"I'm sure," she said softly.

He shook his head. "When are you going to admit that you want me as much as I want you?"

Giddy with her victory and the sheer fun of battling wits with Michael all evening, Barrie gazed up at him provocatively. "Oh, I'm willing to admit that," she said airily.

Michael sucked in his breath and stared at her. "You are?"

"Sure." She grinned at him. "I'm just not going to do anything about it."

Seven

As the season premiere week for the network neared, Barrie's and Michael's lives became more and more hectic. They were both in heavy demand, she at the studio for rehearsals, he in the executive suite, where last minute programming decisions were being made from before dawn to well after midnight. Their contact seemed to be limited to quick late night or early morning phone calls that should have given Barrie the space she'd claimed to need.

And yet as the days passed by in a blur of activity, she instead found herself wanting more intimate contact, wanting to discuss the day's events in more detail, wanting even his most casual touch. Ironically, considering how she'd reacted to his previous comments about the show, she even found herself wanting more of his incisive, clear advice. And to her thorough dismay, just as Danielle had suggested, she also yearned for his enthusiastic approval.

What she didn't want anymore were dictatorial memos and, to her relief, there weren't any. The final script for the first show had zipped through without a murmur of dissent, and the taping was scheduled for the next night, with the premiere episode to air the following week. Her simmering resentment of Michael's arrogant interference had faded without new edicts to fuel it.

In the meantime, there was the benefit gala to which he'd promised to escort her as a respite from their frantic schedules. It began to loom as a monumental turning point in their relationship. For the first time at a lavish, highly visible Hollywood function, she and Michael would be seen as a couple. She knew it would be the stuff people would gossip about the following morning and, as she dressed, she worried over her gown, her shoes, her makeup, even her underwear.

"You're being ridiculous," she muttered, as she tried to decide between two pairs of bikini briefs, one creamy white and mostly lace, the other silky champagne…what there was of it. "The paparazzi will not be taking pictures of your underwear."

It was a comforting thought, but it didn't help her make up her mind. When she realized that her choice would be the only garment, other than the sheer nylons, that she would be wearing under her slinky gown, she grew even more nervous and indecisive. She eyed the glittering copper-colored dress skeptically. The neckline was demure enough in front. It was the back that dipped low to the waist. There was also a provocative slit from the hem to just above her knees. The dress was stunningly sexy, enough to draw women's envy and to turn a man into a lustful beast, according to the saleslady. She humphed at the memory of the woman's own envious gaze. That should have warned her. This was no dress to be wearing with Michael. The man's sexual appetite was legendary, and he'd already made it abundantly clear that he'd like to make her his next meal. Why the devil was she tempting him to take the first bite?

Because some very perverse part of her obviously wanted him to, she told herself dryly. Her body had been sending very clear signals on that point, even when her mind was most vocal in its opposition. Right now her mind was telling her to get out some sedate little black dress, even as she was slipping the coppery designer gown over her head. Another victory for the hormones, she thought with a sigh as she gazed at herself in the mirror.

Her lips curved upward in a pleased smile. The elegant, glamorous woman who stared back at her was a far cry from the terrified teenager who'd left Ohio determined to break the bonds with her past. On the surface that girl had appeared to be afraid of her own shadow, but an inner resilience had driven her, had made her succeed in a profession in which all too many failed. Her shy smile had hidden a toughness that she'd learned from her mother. She had taken the early knocks in a highly competitive profession and turned them to her advantage, learning everything she could about television from anyone who had something to teach.

And, she vowed, she would learn from Michael, as well. When this infatuation of his faded, she would be left with something real, something more lasting than ephemeral love. Love was like a will-o'-the-wisp, elusive and fleeting. A career was tangible, something over which she had some control. She was neither cold nor calculating, but she was a realist. She would not let his dazzling, seductive promises distort her priorities.

For tonight, though, she had every intention of basking in his caressing gaze, of reveling in the warmth of his touch. When she opened the door for him at last and saw his eyes light with a very masculine appreciation, she felt wonderfully special. To be sure, other women in Hollywood were more beautiful than she, but she doubted any of them had ever felt more alluring.

"You are . . . gorgeous," he said softly. "Let me see all of you."

As she spun around, he whistled. "I'm not sure I want to share you with the world. I think I'd like to keep you all to myself."

Barrie's laughter sparkled as brightly as the topaz and diamond earrings that glittered on her ears. "Oh, no, you don't, Mr. Compton. I won the bet fair and square, and we are going out on the town. I've never been to one of these fancy shindigs before."

"They're boring."

"How can a show that features some of the best actors, musicians, dancers and comedians in the country be boring?"

He cocked a brow at her. "My dear," he said as though greatly scandalized by her question, "no one goes to a benefit gala for the show."

"Oh?"

"Of course not. They go to be seen. We are a very generous people out here, but we want to be sure the whole world knows about it."

Barrie glowered at him and shook her head. "And you think my show is too cynical."

Michael smiled one of his soft romantic-album-cover smiles, and her pulse pounded. "Just watch when we get there," he suggested dryly. "You will see more jockeying for position than you've ever seen on the track at Santa Anita."

"You, of course, are just an interested observer of this process?" she retorted lightly. "A sort of self-appointed social commentator?"

"Absolutely."

She grinned up at him and gazed pointedly in the direction of her driveway. "And that's why you rented the limousine?"

"I did not rent it," he responded indignantly. "The network provides it. I just rarely use it."

"I see," she said wryly. "Only on special occasions."

"Exactly."

She flashed him a dazzling, satisfied smile. "When you want to be seen."

He chuckled. "No, you little minx. When I want to have my hands free for the beautiful woman by my side."

Barrie's triumphant smile promptly faded as a flurry of butterfly wings stirred in her abdomen. "Oh."

"That's it? Just oh?" he taunted, mimicking her.

"I think that's sufficient. Besides, with my foot in my mouth, it's difficult to use too many words."

"You mean I've rendered you speechless? Quick, let's go while I have this tremendous advantage."

As they approached the car, the driver stepped out and opened the door for them. Barrie sank down onto the luxurious cushions and glanced around. "I think I could get used to this. Since you don't use it, do you suppose you could have someone start picking me up for work?"

"Sure," he said agreeably, then added casually, "If you leave from my place."

"Never mind."

"I had a feeling you'd say that," he said with exaggerated disappointment. "Too bad. How about a drink?"

He poured them each a glass of champagne. "To us," he said softly, tapping his crystal goblet against hers as he gazed unblinkingly into her eyes. It was as though he were willing her to repeat the toast, to vow with him that they were a couple with a future.

"To us," she murmured at last, unable to resist the power of that steady gaze, the implication of that simple toast.

When they had each sipped the bubbling wine, he took the glass from her. "And now, how about a kiss to seal it?"

"Seal what?"

"Our deal."

"Have we made a deal?" Barrie asked innocently, though her heart thudding against her ribs told her that they had.

He nodded. "You know we have."

He was close, so close she could feel the whisper of his breath against her cheek, feel the heat emanating from his body beneath the tuxedo that made him look even more dashing and desirable than ever. His eyes clung to hers as his hand reached out to skim across her breasts. Beneath the shimmering fabric they peaked into sensitive, aching buds.

"Do you know how I've longed to do that, Barrie MacDonald?" he whispered huskily. His fingers played against the tips, taunted them until a soft moan rumbled in Barrie's throat. "You like that, don't you? I can see it in your eyes."

Barrie wanted to blink and look away, wanted to shutter her eyes against their apparent betrayal, but she couldn't. It was as though the softly-spoken, urgent words and his compelling gaze had hypnotized her. She would have done anything he asked of her. And he had asked for only a kiss.

She leaned toward him, closed the infinitesimal gap and touched his lips gently, praying for nothing more than a sharp tug of heightened awareness. Instead, it was as though a match had been struck and touched to dry tinder. Fiery, all-encompassing, ravishing. She felt herself pulled into his arms, felt his hands skimming down the bare curve of her spine, his touch alternately light and provocative, then rough and possessive. Both of them inflamed her. The innocent kiss he had sought was no longer innocent, had probably never been. He had known—as she should have—that once they were in each other's arms, the pent-up passion that had teased and taunted them would erupt into a full-fledged conflagration.

Barrie was pressed back into the cushions with Michael's body pressed against hers, his weight and warmth welcome rather than oppressive. Her hands had slipped inside the jacket of his tux, seeking bare flesh, but forced to find satisfaction in the muted suggestion of suppleness beneath the fine fabric of his shirt.

"I knew you would be like this," he murmured against her lips. "I knew there were fire and ice. So much sensuality.

"Ahh, Barrie." His tongue flicked against her lips, circled them, then penetrated the opening she gladly gave him. His hand found the opening slit in her dress, gently caressed her thigh, slowly reached upward. Barrie tensed with anticipation and, perhaps, just a hint of dread. The assault on her senses was already unerringly successful. How much further could she allow him to go before she would fall completely under his spell, give herself up to him and to these wonderful blood-stirring sensations?

A subtle cough saved her from having to answer that question.

"Sir, we have arrived." The disembodied voice came to them over the car's intercom.

Reluctantly Michael pulled away from her, his breathing heavy, his face suffused with unfulfilled desire. His hand remained where it had been on her inner thigh, and he caught her gaze and held it.

"I must be a mess," Barrie muttered, wanting to look away in embarrassment.

He grinned at her. "You look like a woman who has just been thoroughly kissed. The photographers will have a field day."

He started to climb out the door, which the driver had just opened.

Barrie grabbed his arm and held him back. "Michael," she whispered urgently. "I can't get out of here looking like this."

"Of course, you can. You look beautiful."

She looked at him oddly. "You really don't mind what people think, do you?"

"Why should I? I'm not ashamed of our relationship."

He gave her a penetrating look. "Are you?"

"No. Of course not."

"Then let's get out of here and prove my point about why all these people have come."

As they exited the car, flashbulbs popped, and several reporters asked Michael questions about the upcoming television season. He fielded them with absolute aplomb. He didn't even wince when one of the reporters asked, with a pointed glance at Barrie, if he thought *Goodbye, Again* would be given more than the usual amount of time to prove itself.

thrilled only to the chase, and admittedly, at the moment she was leading him on a merry one. Once the intrigue of that chase had ended, would he vanish, leaving her to nurse her pain as her father had so often left her mother?

Of course he would. Even now, though he drew her into the conversation, sought her opinions and listened respectfully, chuckled at her wit, she alone knew how easily he could turn on her, cut her down to size. When push came to shove, she felt her opinions didn't matter one whit to him.

They were both too strong-minded, too stubborn for this to work. Perhaps if their professional lives weren't intertwined, they would have been ideally suited. She could envision the challenge of late-night conversations during which they would hone their intelligence, spar over everything from the Star Wars arms race to the social satire of *Doonesbury*. She could imagine the passionate lovemaking that would be sparked by such lively debates, such diversity of opinion.

But that was the fantasy. The reality was something entirely different. The reality was Michael arguing with her over the actions of her characters, changing and distorting her dreams. The devastating possibility was that Michael would end up snatching her career just when it was within her grasp. She would hate him for that, even though she might understand it rationally. And it would destroy them.

She sighed as his fingers massaged the sensitive spot at the base of her spine. Her troubled eyes met his questioning gaze.

"What's wrong?"

"Nothing," she denied.

"Why don't I believe that?"

"Beats me," she retorted bravely. "I'm having a terrific time."

"But?"

She grimaced at his perceptiveness and his persistence. "But I think I'd better get home. Tomorrow's a busy day."

He grinned at her. "Do I sense a thank goodness at the end of that sentence?"

She gave an embarrassed chuckle. "Well..."

"It's okay. Sooner or later, you're going to stop running, Barrie MacDonald. And when you do, I'm going to be right there."

"Is that a threat?"

"Nope," he said softly. "A promise."

Eight

As soon as the closing shot of the first episode of
Goodbye, Again had been taped, and the audience's
enthusiastic applause was nothing more than a fading
echo in the studio, Barrie heaved a sigh of relief and
slipped out of the control booth. It had gone reasonably well, far better tonight than during the previous
night's dress rehearsal. The audience had been responsive, the laughs had come in all the right places,
and Melinda had been absolutely superb as Karen
Devereaux. Even if the show failed, she would emerge
with a solid reputation as a talented comedic actress,
a true television star. Barrie was sure of it.

"You were all magnificent," she praised as the
weary troupe virtually collapsed in the vacated studio. "I think a party is in order. When we go on the air

next week, I want you all to come to my place for a celebration bash. You deserve it. I think we're going to have a hit."

"Do you really believe that we can make it even in this time slot?" Danielle asked quietly with a look of pure wide-eyed innocence.

Barrie's brows shot up in horrified disbelief. She wasn't particularly shocked by her friend's question, only by the fact that she had voiced it tactlessly in front of the others on what should have been their big night to celebrate. Now, instead of excitement, their faces suddenly registered uncertainty. It was one of the few times she had ever known Danielle to display such lousy timing. Barrie tried quickly to undo the apparently unwitting damage.

"I believe this show is intelligent, witty and unique," she said with heartfelt conviction, staring pointedly at Danielle as though daring her to disagree. "I'm convinced the critics and the audience will find it."

Her comment effectively silenced Danielle, but not Heath. "Assuming they aren't all out at the movies," he muttered bitterly, echoing Danielle's concern and reinforcing the depressing atmosphere.

"Don't think that way," Barrie chided him. "We are not going into this with a defeatist attitude. If we don't believe in ourselves, we'll never convince anyone else. Remember, *All in the Family* and *Hill Street Blues* weren't hits when they first went on the air, either. They took time to build an audience, and they did it by word of mouth and critical acclaim. We can do the same thing."

"Sure. But like you said yourself, first they have to find us," he retorted, oblivious to the increasingly dismayed stares of the exhausted and increasing appalled cast. But when Barrie glared at him, he finally caught on to the effect his words were having, especially on the younger members of the cast and crew who hadn't been around long enough to become used to the mercurial nature of working in television.

"Oh, all right. I'll shut up," he grumbled.

"Thank you," she replied with exaggerated sweetness. "Now stop worrying and get out of here, guys. We have a new show to work on beginning Monday."

Depressed by her admittedly ineffective attempt at a pep talk, Barrie started slowly back to her office.

"You're furious with me, aren't you?" Danielle said, walking along with her.

"No," she said tiredly. "Not really. I was surprised, but I'm sure you only said what everyone else was thinking. I suppose it was better to get it out in the open."

"I thought so," Danielle said. "They needed to hear that you still believe in them and in the show."

Barrie looked at her in astonishment. "You set me up, didn't you?"

Danielle grinned. "Something like that. I just wanted to be sure they got the message that no matter what happens in the ratings they've done their best, and the show really is great. I figured you're the only one they'd believe."

"I guess I ought to thank you."

"That would be nice, but I'll settle for your company at dinner."

Barrie shook her head. "Not tonight, Dani. I want to look over next week's script one last time."

"You sure you're not holding out for a better offer?" Danielle inquired hopefully.

"No. I just need some time to myself," she said vaguely. It was a flimsy excuse, but it seemed to satisfy Danielle, who left after giving her a quick hug and some sage advice about what she ought to be doing with the rest of her evening. As usual, it involved Michael and speeding up the snail's pace at which their relationship was progressing.

When she was alone, Barrie tried to push Danielle's very explicit comments from her mind and to focus on the fact that her very first television series was about to go on the air. Her effort failed miserably. While thinking of her series' debut should have thrilled her, it had become so intertwined with her personal relationship with Michael that she was more confused than excited. She'd been trying all week to blame her odd sense of disorientation on the pressure of finishing the show, but she knew it was more than that. Thanks to Michael, she was on an emotional merry-go-round and had no idea how to get off.

But, instead of having time to think, no sooner had she settled down behind her desk than the phone rang. She knew intuitively that it was Michael.

"How did it go?" he asked without preamble.

"Are you asking personally, or do you want an analysis that will soothe a worried network programmer?"

"Both."

"The audience seemed to like it. The pacing was fine. Danielle did a superb job. The cast was terrific."

"And you? What do you think?"

She hesitated, then finally admitted with total honesty. "I'm worried sick."

"Why?"

"You know why. You've put us in an impossible time slot."

"If the show's as good as you say it is, the ratings will be there."

"You know better than that."

"Barrie, if I didn't have faith in this show, I wouldn't have put it where I did," he said sincerely.

"Do you mean that?"

"Of course, I mean it. Why would you doubt it?"

"I thought perhaps you were making it your sacrificial lamb, because you figured it didn't have a prayer, anyway."

"Hey, what's this?" he said softly, the soothing tone like a balm to her opening night jitters. "What's happening to that upbeat, confident producer who keeps telling me how terrific her series is?"

"She's getting cold feet."

"Want to meet me tonight and let me warm them up?" he suggested huskily.

The invitation held an incredible appeal, an irresistible appeal, in fact, and not just because of Danielle's earlier nudging. She needed someone tonight, someone who would bolster her flagging spirits, someone who would make her feel warm and secure. She denied that what she really needed was Michael and that only he could make her feel that way. She still wanted desperately to believe that anyone would do.

"Why not?" she said boldly. She heard Michael gasp in surprise.

"Sure?"

"I'm sure."

"I'll meet you at your place in an hour, then. I just have a few things to wrap up here."

"See you," she said softly, a flutter of anticipation skittering along her nerves.

She threw the script into her briefcase, ran to her car and made the drive to Santa Monica in forty-five minutes. She barely had time to straighten up the living room, change the towels in the bathroom and freshen her makeup before Michael was ringing the doorbell impatiently. Fortunately, she had no time to reconsider her decision to let him come over, or she might have panicked. Instead she took a deep breath and opened the door.

"Hi," she said, struck by an unexpected shyness as she surveyed him from head to toe, taking in the perfectly tailored brown suit, beige shirt and pin-striped tie. Once more, she admired the way he always managed to look as though he'd just modeled for the cover of a magazine even after a fifteen-hour day. Only his thick brown hair was less than perfect. It was wind-blown, as though he'd driven over with the car windows rolled down to catch the cool breeze. It made him look healthier and more attractive than ever. She, on the other hand, felt limp and exhausted and suspected she looked it, as well. If he still wanted her after seeing her like this, she had a feeling she ought to grab him and hang on for dear life.

"Hi, yourself," he said, brushing a gentle, undemanding kiss across her lips and pushing a stunningly wrapped package into her hands. He barely looked at her.

"What's this?"

"A present," he said vaguely, prowling around the living room as though he'd been sent on a scouting expedition. He studied the titles of the books on her shelves, picked up the pictures she had scattered about, glanced out her windows. He even picked up her stack of unopened mail and thumbed through it. He did all of this without saying another word or even looking at her. Barrie couldn't decide whether to be amused or irritated.

"Are you searching for something in particular?" she finally inquired with exaggerated politeness. "Maybe I can help."

"What?" Michael asked distractedly, now seemingly absorbed by the cover story of a business magazine.

"I asked if you were looking for something."

"No, not really."

"Just hunting up more clues for my personnel file, then?"

He grinned at her sheepishly. "Nope. I think that's pretty well up-to-date."

Barrie looked at him oddly. "Michael Compton, are you nervous?" she asked incredulously.

"Me? Of course not," he retorted indignantly.

"You are, too. I would never have believed it."

"Open your present."

"Don't try to change the subject. Why are you so uptight?"

Michael sighed and kept pacing. "It's your fault, you know."

"What's my fault?"

"You keep sending out these conflicting signals, so that I'm never quite sure from one minute to the next where we stand. Tonight on the phone I thought I got a very clear message, but now that I'm here, I'm not so sure. You seem distant again."

Barrie put the package down on the sofa and moved closer to him. "I'm sorry," she said softly. "Would it help if I told you that I haven't known from one minute to the next where we stand, either?"

"And tonight?"

She took a deep breath and gazed unblinkingly into his eyes. Tentative fingers reached up to touch his lips, caress the firm line of his jaw. His eyes darkened with passion at her touch, and a muscle in his neck twitched with the effort of restraint as he waited for her to speak.

"Tonight I want to be with you," she said honestly. "I need you. I need your warmth and your sensitivity and . . . and your loving."

"Oh, Barrie," he said, drawing her into his arms then and just holding her, letting her feel his strength, the power of his desire. Her head nestled into the curve of his neck, and when he whispered huskily of his need for her, the words ruffled her hair and sent tiny shocks tripping along her spine. His body trembled in her arms, and she realized for the first time how deeply she affected him. What's more, she realized how very much she needed him.

Her openness about her need, her commitment that whatever else happened tonight would be theirs seemed to remove some of the pressure. There was no urgency, only a deep sense of the rightness of this moment. They moved to the sofa and sat cuddled together and talked of their lives and dreams, of hopes and possibilities, of past adventures and future plans. They talked through the night and at dawn, with the sun streaking the sky with pale golden light, they made love, their passion gentled into something beautiful and tender, something that was totally giving.

Theirs was no fumbling first-time exploration. It was as though their bodies had been made for each other, as though they knew instinctively exactly how to please, where to touch, what to say, when to hold back. Her small, high breasts fit perfectly into the warm palm of his hand. His fingers sparked an exquisite tension as they played over her inner thighs, then moved slowly upward seeking her moist warmth. Michael's skin under her touch was supple and responsive, his rock-hard thighs everything she had dreamed of. Her lips explored the intriguing contradictions of his body, the hairy roughness of his chest and legs, the smoothness of his flat stomach. Her tongue tasted the tangy saltiness of his flesh.

For the first time in her life, Barrie found that she was unafraid of sharing herself completely and without reservation. And in that sharing she discovered a height of ecstasy never reached before. Michael's whispered words excited her, his touch against the satin of her flesh inflamed her, but more than that, his joyous release sent her own senses spiraling out of control. She gave herself up to an abandoned wantonness that provoked him, teased him and ultimately satisfied him beyond measure. Apart, they were strong and good and fiercely independent. Together, there seemed to be no limits to what they could feel, where they could soar.

"I just have one question, Miss MacDonald," Michael murmured huskily as they lay in each other's arms with sunlight dappling their flesh with a patchwork of brightness. "Why did we take so long to get here?"

"Because you're a gentleman," she retorted.

"I beg your pardon?"

"Most other men would not have been nearly as patient as you've been," she told him candidly.

He lifted himself to one elbow and gazed at her incredulously. One hand lay possessively on the curve of her waist, a curve he had explored in erotic detail during their lovemaking and now cupped with a lover's sure knowledge. "Are you telling me that if I'd thrown you over my shoulder and dragged you to bed, I could have avoided all those damn cold showers I took?"

She grinned at him impishly and wriggled under his roving fingers. "Probably."

Michael moaned.

"But," she added soothingly, "I would have hated you in the morning."

"Ahh. I see. And this morning?"

"This morning I am feeling so benevolent toward you that I might even consider fixing you some breakfast before you leave."

"Before I leave?" he repeated in amazement. "Woman, are you some kind of a sadist? I've been up all night. I need sleep. I don't need a cup of coffee, some toast and a long drive on the freeway."

She patted his shoulder. "You'll rest much better in your own bed."

"And you?"

"I'll rest much better in my own bed—" she paused, then added firmly "—alone."

"Why does that confuse me?"

Barrie shrugged. "It shouldn't."

"Are we back to playing games?"

She gazed at him with serious brown eyes. "Michael, I have never played games with you. I've told you from the beginning that it couldn't work between us."

Puzzlement suddenly filled his eyes. "Then what was last night all about?"

"Last night was about two mature adults who needed each other."

Confusion changed to hurt, then anger. "That's all it was for you? I don't believe it. You wanted me, Barrie. Me, Michael. Not just some willing male body."

Barrie winced at the accusatory tone, the underlying plea for an acknowledgment of caring that she wasn't prepared to make. Last night...this morning...had been special, but that didn't mean anything. She wouldn't let it. She would send Michael on his way and tug her defensive cloak back into place. It had slipped during the long, tender night, but she hadn't completely lost it.

"Michael, please," she begged softly. "Don't do this. I loved what we shared. I just don't want to magnify it all out of proportion."

Michael drew in a shocked breath, then exploded, "That is the most ridiculous comment I have ever heard in my life! You know we have something special between us, something the whole world searches for and hardly ever finds. Why won't you admit it?"

"I can't," she said simply. "It's not real."

Her cool words seemed to incense him. He grabbed her roughly and pulled her into his arms. His lips against hers were hot, demanding, his hands possessive, sure. Barrie felt yet another stirring of excitement, as flames licked through her. She tried to pull away, but he wouldn't release her. His body next to hers was on fire, his arousal pressing against her thigh with a powerful, tantalizing intimacy. A shudder of dismay seemed to rack his body and then, at last, he pushed her away, as though half-afraid of where his anger might lead. He looked shattered.

"Was that real enough for you?" he demanded, leaping out of bed and picking up his scattered clothes. He slammed the bathroom door shut behind him, and Barrie heard the shower go on. It seemed to pound down with the unrelenting fury of a storm. She couldn't bear listening to it another minute, imagining Michael's naked body standing under the harsh spray tense with outrage.

Barrie put on her robe and padded into the kitchen, her heart still thudding against her ribs. His violence hadn't really scared her. She had known instinctively that Michael would never harm her. But the depth of his anger had shaken her. A sophisticated male was supposed to kiss and say goodbye with calm acceptance. In fact, most of them were absolutely delighted to discover that their night's partner had no designs on their future independence. Why had Michael reacted so differently? Was it possible he actually cared about her?

She fumbled with the coffee maker with fingers made shaky by lack of sleep and tension. She spilled her first spoonful of coffee all over the counter and finally managed to get the machine working properly. By the time Michael came into the living room, she was sitting on the sofa, sipping a cup of very strong coffee. She looked up at him wearily.

He raked his fingers through his still-damp hair, the brown tendrils falling haphazardly onto his brow, giving him an appealingly boyish appearance. But there was nothing boyish or innocent about his anguish. "Please don't look at me like that," he begged contritely. "I'm sorry, I was furious, but I had no right to take it out on you like that."

Barrie returned his gaze with a thoughtful, unwavering look. "Maybe you did," she admitted at last. "Last night was important to you, wasn't it?"

"Of course it was important. I care about you. I've wanted to be with you for weeks now. Last night was just the way I knew it would be with us."

"Then I'm sorry if you thought I was demeaning it. I didn't mean to. It was special for me, too."

"Really?"

"Really." She paused, then added slowly, "But now I need some distance."

She looked up at him hopefully. "Can you try to understand that?"

He sighed, but nodded. "I can try, but you're not giving me many clues."

"I can't. I don't have it all straight in my head yet."

"Then I guess I'll have to wait."

"I'll call you later," she offered. "If you want me to."

"I want you to."

He gazed at her tenderly once again, the blue-green of his eyes shadowed with desire once more. "I'd better get out of here, or my noble promises won't be worth a hoot."

Barrie started to stand to walk him to the door. He waved her back.

"Don't move. I want to leave with the image of you curled up in the corner of the sofa like that. You look like a sleepy, contented cat."

"'Night, Michael."

"It's morning, love." He stood in the doorway for several long minutes, just staring at her, then smiled. "Sleep well."

After he had gone, Barrie opened the present that had been left, forgotten, on the coffee table. It was a leather-bound copy of the script for the opening episode of *Goodbye, Again*. She clutched the thoughtful gift to her and tried to blink back her tears.

Michael's sensitivity, his touching generosity never ceased to surprise her. He was trying so hard to understand, but what he said was true. She wasn't giving him many clues, and he deserved them. It was even more than that. He deserved not just clues, but clear, straightforward answers.

She vowed to search her heart and find them for him.

For both of them.

Nine

————

"What's he doing here?" Heath hissed as Barrie's front door swung open to admit Michael to the cast's already boisterous celebration of their premiere night.

"Shut up," Danielle muttered. "Barrie invited him."

"Nothing like bringing the enemy into the middle of your camp."

"Do you know a better way to disarm him?" she responded reasonably. "Besides, Barrie cares about him."

"Then she's crazier than I'd ever imagined," Heath snapped back. "The man's a... Oh, forget it. I'm going out on the patio."

"I think that's probably a good idea."

Barrie overheard the biting remarks, but she was too engrossed in greeting Michael to care much about the impact of his arrival on Heath and the others. She had known some of them wouldn't be overjoyed to have him here, but it was her party, and she wanted to see him, wanted to share this special night with him.

They had talked only a few times in the past week. Apparently he had taken her request for distance to heart and had given her all that she wanted. More, in fact. He hadn't called her once, waiting instead for her to call him. She'd never felt so lonely or abandoned in her life. After the decree she'd uttered only a few days earlier, she'd decided it was wiser not to try to figure out why she felt that way. As usual, though, Danielle had not been above offering a few pointed observations on the subject.

To Barrie's dismay, she was beginning to believe her friend might be right. At the very least, she had admitted to herself that she was clearly infatuated with Michael. Probably more than infatuated. Whatever label she stuck on it didn't really matter. The important thing was that she had decided to put aside her doubts, to open herself up to the possibilities of the relationship. No longer would she hold him at arm's length. Her newfound resolve gave a special warmth to her welcoming smile.

"I'm glad you came," she said, gazing up at him with brightly shining eyes no longer hidden behind glasses. Her new contacts had finally arrived, and she could actually see clearly just how spectacular he looked in his jeans and formfitting knit shirt.

Michael surveyed the gathering of hostile faces and grinned at her. "You're probably the only one."

"Ahh, but it's my party. I'm the only one who counts."

"You're the only one who counts with me, anyway."

"Let me get you a drink, and then you can mingle."

He feigned horror. "Mingle? With this crowd? They'll tear me to pieces. I thought you said you were glad to see me."

"I am. Very," she said softly, tucking her arm through his. "But I'm also the hostess. I have things to do."

"What things?"

She grinned at him and said airily, "Oh, you know. Hostessy things."

"Maybe I can help."

"Watch it, Mr. Compton," Danielle warned, coming up to wrap an arm around Barrie's waist. "She'll have you in the kitchen wearing a frilly apron and chopping up bits of disgusting raw chicken livers, if you're not careful."

"Chicken livers?" he repeated, eyeing Barrie skeptically. "Maybe I'll just stay here and talk to your talented director."

Barrie sniffed. "Oh, no you don't. You offered to help. Danielle abandoned me, just because I asked her to make a few little hors d'oeuvres."

"I did not sign on to touch that stuff," she said with an exaggerated shiver. "Ugh."

"You eat *that stuff*," Barrie reminded her.

"Of course. But that's after it's been wrapped around a water chestnut, surrounded by bacon and broiled beyond recognition. If I'd had any idea what it looked like in its natural state, I'd never have touched it."

Barrie laughed. "Okay, you win. You two enjoy yourselves. I'll do KP all by myself."

Michael and Danielle exchanged a significant look. "Does that sound like the wounded cry of a martyr to you?" he asked.

"Unfortunately, yes," she replied resignedly. "I suppose we both had better help, or we'll never hear the end of it."

The three of them worked side by side in the kitchen, finishing up the preparation of the appetizers and stirring the big pot of chili Barrie had made the day before. Michael kept adding chili powder whenever Barrie's back was turned. When she finally caught him at it and sampled the resulting spicy stew, her eyes watered, and she grabbed for a glass of ice water.

"What have you done?" she finally choked out between gulps of cooling liquid that did nothing to soothe her throat but pacified her need to do something.

"It needed a little oomph!" he informed her cheerfully. "Is it better now?"

"Better? It's lethal," she sputtered. "Do you realize that half those guests in there probably have ulcers already? This stuff will kill them."

Danielle dished up a spoonful and tasted it. "Umm," she said approvingly. "Barrie, what are you grumbling about? This is just right."

"Thank you," Michael said with exaggerated appreciation, then stared pointedly at Barrie. "See."

Barrie shuddered. "Okay, you two. I hold you responsible for calling the ambulances when those people start writhing on the floor."

"Don't mind her," Danielle told Michael airily. "She has always been a culinary wimp. In college she once complained to the cafeteria manager that the gravy was too spicy. Can you imagine ever calling that bland, awful glue too spicy?"

"That is not true, Danielle Lawrence."

"Well, it was something like that."

Danielle was not the least bit intimidated by Barrie's outraged protest. Her irreverent—and, according to Barrie, greatly exaggerated—tales of Barrie's college antics kept them all howling, until finally Heath and Melinda stuck their heads in the door to find out what was going on. They looked like two kids who were feeling left out of all the fun.

"Hey, you guys," Melinda said. "The party's out here. You're not supposed to be enjoying yourselves over the drudgery."

"What drudgery?" Danielle asked with feigned perplexity. "I thought Barrie had come up with a new party game."

"In that case, who's winning?" Heath demanded.

"I think I am," Michael confessed. "I'm in here with two beautiful women all to myself."

"Maybe you should make it three," Melinda suggested with coy seductiveness.

"I think I'm in over my head with just the two of them, but what the heck," he responded gallantly. "Come on in."

"Actually I think you all should get out here," Heath interjected. "The show's coming on in just a couple of minutes."

In the living room everyone had gathered around the large-screen set by the time Barrie and Michael and the others came in. Barrie found a spot on the floor, and Michael sat right behind her. She leaned back against his chest, liking the comfort that broad, solid expanse offered her. One hand rested on his leg. His very muscular, very tempting leg. Her other hand kept creeping toward her mouth as she fought unsuccessfully against the temptation to bite her nails.

For the next half hour the group chuckled as they saw themselves on the air, laughing at Heath's clever dialogue and grinning as Melinda's Karen kept Mason decisively at arm's length, while taunting him with veiled promises. Barrie listened closely for Michael's laughter, cringed when it didn't come on cue, beamed with satisfaction when it did. As caught up as she was in the pride of creation, though, she knew there was something missing. It wasn't only Michael's tautness that told her that. She sensed it instinctively. There was a critical beat missing, some elusive ingredient that they would have to find if the characters were to blend perfectly.

At the end, when the others were congratulating each other, she gazed into Michael's face, saw the internal struggle he waged to find words that wouldn't hurt her, wouldn't hurt any of them.

"It was bad, wasn't it?" she asked softly, so the others couldn't hear.

"No." He shook his head. "It wasn't bad. The characters are good. The concept is good. The performances were great."

"But something's missing."

"Yes."

"Any idea what it is?"

"Nope. I can't quite put my finger on it."

"Neither can I."

He gave her a quick kiss. "Let's not worry about it tonight. Tonight we'll celebrate, and next week we'll take a look at the show more closely. I don't want us to throw a damper on your party."

From that moment on, it was as though *Goodbye, Again* hadn't even aired. Michael did his best to put the others guests at ease, to make them forget he was a network vice president. He showed them his warmth, his humor and, most of all, he was obvious about his deep affection for their producer. As protective as they all were of each other, that alone would have endeared him to them. By the end of the evening, Barrie noted, even Heath had mellowed.

"He hasn't called me a cretin once," Michael whispered triumphantly to Barrie when they were alone in the kitchen sipping cups of coffee.

She looked at him incredulously. "You knew he'd called you that?"

"Of course."

"Kevin, I suppose."

"A network executive never reveals his sources."

"I thought that was reporters."

"Them, too." He nuzzled her neck. "Do you suppose these friends of yours would be offended if I suggested it was time for them to leave?"

"Probably."

"What about if you told them?"

"Why would I want to do that?" she taunted impishly.

"So you can run your hands over my incredible thighs," he murmured with a wicked gleam in his eyes.

Barrie's mouth dropped open, and she flushed with embarrassment. "You know about that, too?"

He nodded.

"I think I'll order a closed set first thing Monday morning."

"Won't work," he told her seriously. "My spies are everywhere."

"Danielle again," she muttered in disgust. "What am I going to do with her?"

"Treasure her. She's a terrific friend."

"I'm not so sure."

"Who's a terrific friend?" the woman in question inquired tartly, sticking her head in the door.

"You are." Michael confirmed, just as Barrie responded "Nobody."

Danielle gazed from one to the other, her sharp eyes missing nothing. Barrie knew that she had witnessed their growing closeness, measured it and approved wholeheartedly. She also guessed she would connive to encourage it. Her next comment proved it.

"I just wanted to let you know that I've nudged everyone else out of here," she announced proudly. "They all said thanks and good-night."

"See what I mean?" Michael murmured, nibbling on Barrie's ear. "She's a jewel."

"Notice that she hasn't left yet," Barrie reminded him significantly.

"I'm on my way. See you two on Monday," she said breezily. She winked at Michael. "Have a wonderful night."

"Goodbye, Danielle," Barrie said firmly.

"What about me?" Michael inquired when they were alone. "Do I go or stay?"

"What do you want to do?"

"You know the answer to that."

"Then I'd say you should follow your instincts."

The rest of the weekend passed in a wonderfully tender, sensual blur. It was a time for new discoveries, for more talk, long walks on the beach and passionate lovemaking. This time Barrie did not pull away afterward. Instead she hugged Michael to her and held on, delighting in this newfound excitement that rocked her senses, the tenderness that touched her heart, the matching of wits that brought them ever closer.

By Tuesday, though, the memory of those moments of mental and emotional intimacy had dimmed, replaced by new concerns over *Goodbye, Again*. When the ratings for the premiere came in during the week, Barrie felt shell-shocked as she stared at the national Neilsen numbers. She had anticipated problems because of the time slot but nothing like this.

Better to confront Michael about this head-on, she decided. She was just reaching for the phone to call him when it rang.

"Hello, dear. It's Mrs. Hastings. Mr. Compton would like to see you, Mr. Donaldson and Miss Lawrence in his office."

"When?" Barrie asked with a sense of dread, wishing she'd had a chance to initiate the meeting on her own terms.

"As soon as you can get here."

"We're in the middle of a rehearsal."

"I know, dear, but I think he wants you here now, anyway." She paused, and Barrie thought she could hear Michael's voice in the background. When Mrs. Hastings came back on the line, she confirmed it. "He said immediately, Miss MacDonald."

Barrie sighed. "Okay. We'll be right there."

This was not going to be pleasant. If Michael hadn't even called her himself, he must be in quite a state of agitation. Whatever doubts he had had on Saturday night must have been solidified by the low ratings. Quickly she rounded up Heath and Danielle, and they walked across to the executive tower together. Barrie had a rough idea of what it must have felt like to walk to the guillotine.

"You don't suppose he'd cancel us after just a week," Danielle said, anticipating the worst.

"Of course not," Barrie said with far more conviction than she felt. "I'm sure he just wants to try to figure out some new game plan. Maybe he'll even see how right we were about the time period and move us."

"Don't hold your breath," Heath muttered, his defensiveness back in place.

Once they were in Michael's office, Barrie knew that her optimism had been unfounded. Michael's expression teetered somewhere between serious and ominous. To top it off, he hadn't even glanced in her direction, as though he found the idea of a direct confrontation with her over this too uncomfortable after all they had shared over the weekend.

"We have a problem," he announced without preamble.

Barrie took a deep breath and plunged in before he could go on. "Michael, I'm sure if we just give the show a little promotional push, it will begin picking up," she said with bravado. "I've already talked to the PR department, and they're going to set up some interviews for Melinda. On-air promotion says they'll get some spots on during football. That's always good exposure for a new series."

"That's all great, but it's not the answer."

"And I suppose you have one," Heath murmured belligerently. "Are we back to that blasted sheepdog again?"

Michael chuckled. "No, no sheepdog. But I think we are going to have to make some changes in the show, do a little fine-tuning with the characters." When Danielle started to interrupt, he shook his head. "Nothing drastic," he said soothingly.

For the next few minutes he outlined possibilities and asked for their input. For the most part, Barrie found little to disagree with. His comments were incisive and proved that he not only understood what they were trying to do, but that he knew the audience, as well. Heath and Danielle at least seemed relieved by the tone of the conversation. Barrie wasn't quite so certain. She had a feeling the worst was yet to come.

"Now let's talk about Karen," he said at last.

"Karen!" Barrie's voice rose as though the falling ax had just made contact with her neck for the first time. "Karen is just fine."

"No, she isn't," he said adamantly. "She needs to be softer, more vulnerable."

"Forget it," she retorted equally adamantly. "We're not changing Karen."

"Do you want the show to stay on the air?" he asked bluntly.

Barrie blinked and stared at him in amazement. "You would kill this show if I don't agree to let you change Karen's character?"

"Karen is central to *Goodbye, Again*," he said. "Would you agree with that?"

"Of course."

"Then fixing her is critical to making the show work. Without the changes I'm suggesting, you have nothing. You, not I, will be killing the show."

Barrie sank back in her chair in temporary defeat. "What did you want to do?"

"I told you. Make her more vulnerable. I want the audience to care about her. The way she is now, she's too glib, too sophisticated and certain of herself. That must be toned down to make her more appealing."

Suddenly Barrie couldn't take another word, another criticism of the woman who was her own alter ego. She was on her feet, her brown eyes flashing sparks. "Do you think I'm too tough? Too independent?" she demanded, as Danielle murmured a hasty excuse, urged Heath to his feet and practically dragged him out of the room. Barrie wasn't sure whether to bless or curse her for leaving her to deal with Michael alone.

"Of course I don't think you're too tough," Michael responded, clearly perplexed. "What does that have to do with anything?"

"Am I loveable?"

"Don't be absurd. You know how I feel about you. I find your strength, your spunk very appealing. How did we switch from Karen to you?"

"I am Karen. This show is all about me. You know that. You even said it yourself."

"Barrie!"

"No, wait. Every time you chip away at it, every time you want to change something, it's as though you're stripping away a little more of me."

"Is that what all the defensiveness has been about? You think I've been criticizing you?"

"Well, haven't you? You were the one who cut that scene in the premiere because it didn't match what was happening with us. You obviously compared me with Karen yourself."

"I compared the situation and, yes, I suppose I realized that you and Karen had certain similarites. But I had no idea that you identified with her so strongly. I certainly didn't think you'd be so subjective about a character that you'd think I was attacking you."

"Would knowing that have made any difference?"

"In my decisions? No," he said honestly. "But I would have handled this better. I would have tried to make it clear that my comments were not personal in any way, that I was only trying to make the show work."

He sighed deeply. "Sweetheart, we may not always agree on what's best for the show or what an audience will accept at eight o'clock, but that's only a difference of opinion. It's certainly not a reflection of my feelings for you, any more than it would be if I preferred red wine and you preferred white."

"I do prefer white."

A soft smile curved his lips. "I can live with that," he said lightly. His voice became huskier. "In fact, I would like to live with you."

Barrie's mouth fell open. "You can't be serious."

"Of course I'm serious."

"You picked a very strange time to suggest that sort of a step for us."

"I've been thinking about it for weeks now. Hell, I've been thinking about it since the day we met."

"Do you actually think I would live with you when you're in the process of carving my future to bits?"

"Barrie, don't you understand yet? That's professional, not personal."

"Then I guess I'm just not all that liberated. I don't see how you can separate the two."

To her utter chagrin, his blue-green eyes were sparkling with amusement. "Karen could," he suggested pointedly.

"Well, I'm not Karen," she flashed back.

"That's not what you said a minute ago."

Barrie felt as though her world were suddenly spinning crazily. "You ... you ... Oh, why don't you just get out of here?"

"It's my office," he countered, infuriating her with his low chuckle and damnable logic.

"Then I'll go."

He shrugged. "If you must," he taunted. "Just think about what I said."

"I will not live with you, and I will not change Karen," she repeated firmly. "Not in a million years."

As she flounced out of the office, she heard him murmur softly, "We'll see."

Ten

Barrie spent the next couple of days thinking about Michael's taunting comment. He was right. Karen would live with someone if she cared about him as deeply as Barrie was beginning to realize that she cared about Michael. She would accept the relationship for what it was, rejoice in it for however long it lasted, then blithely say goodbye again when it was over. Thanks and no hard feelings. Wasn't that the way modern relationships ended?

When Barrie had developed that easygoing style for Karen, it had seemed so simple and straightforward. It had been based on her own background of honesty and a complete lack of guile, as well as her ability to recognize clearly her own motives and needs and to act on them without any thought of the future. Apparently she had not allowed for the complexity of emotions that surfaced in a relationship of any depth. Certainly, she had not considered the possibility that any opening of the heart, any prolonged contact with a man of substance and sensitivity such as Michael, would create a natural vulnerability.

Based on her own past experience, she had thought a wise contemporary woman could remain aloof and uninvolved even in the most intimate relationship. She realized now what a short-sighted fool she had been! The men she'd known before had made it easy to stay objective and cool, had encouraged it, in fact. But they weren't at all like Michael. They had lacked his depth and certainly had lacked his desire for more serious involvement.

What now? she asked herself more than once. There was no point in denying that she was deeply involved with Michael, more than she had ever been with any other man. But how did he really feel about her? He never said that he loved her, only that he wanted to live with her. Was that enough? According to the standards she'd set for Karen, yes. But what about for her, especially now that she knew she was falling in love with him?

The more she thought about it, the more she realized that the only answer seemed to be to go along with his suggestion, to live with him and see what happened. Hadn't she just resolved to follow the relationship wherever it led? Was she ready to forget that resolution so quickly?

After all, despite her doubts, perhaps they could make it work. They could even discover their true feelings together. As Danielle had noted, Michael was everything she had ever claimed to want in a man. She hadn't often allowed herself to dream of an ideal mate, convinced that such dreams were futile. But during those sleepy late-night conversations she and Danielle had shared in college, she'd been pressed into describing someone who, in retrospect, had sounded very much like Michael. Strong, secure in his sense of himself, supportive, sensitive and funny. Now that she'd found someone like that, did she dare to risk losing him through her own indecision?

The answer was an emphatic no!

Bravely she picked up the phone and dialed Michael's office. "Okay, hotshot," she announced before her confidence could waver. "Let's give it a try."

"Give what a try? The changes?"

"No. Living together."

Michael practically choked, which was not exactly the delighted reaction she'd counted on to reassure her that she'd made the right decision. It was not particularly heartwarming, either. She'd envisioned his eyes darkening with passion as he murmured something like "Oh, darling, you'll never regret this. We'll be happy together. I promise."

Instead he was saying lightly, "Excuse me, are you sure you have the right number? This is the office of Michael Compton, vice president for programming."

She winced. "Don't rub it in."

The teasing didn't let up. "Who is this?" he inquired, his voice filled with exaggerated puzzlement. "I recognize the voice, but the remark seems strangely out of character."

"Cute."

"Is this the woman who only a few short days ago told me to take a flying leap off a Malibu cliff when I suggested this very same thing?"

"I never said any such thing," she retorted defensively, miffed by his thoroughly unromantic attitude. He was making fun of her, treating the most momentous decision of her life as a big joke.

"Maybe not precisely, but words to that effect."

"So I've had a change of heart. I'm entitled," she said stiffly, wondering why she was even bothering to try to convince him of her sincerity. If he weren't interested any longer, her pride told her she ought to forget it, as well. But she couldn't do that now. Not without a fight.

"And you think we should live together?" he was saying with slow deliberation, as though allowing her time to reconsider.

With her heart thundering against her ribs, Barrie ignored his skeptical response to her overture and replied firmly, "Yes."

The word seemed to hang in the midst of a very deadly silence.

"Sorry, angel," he said at last. "I don't fool around."

Suddenly the ground seemed to drop out from beneath her, and her resolve crumbled. This bland disinterest was the last thing she had anticipated. Where on earth had it come from? Only a few short days ago the man had been practically begging her to make a stronger commitment to him. Now, when she'd swallowed her pride, called him and announced that she had come around to his point of view, he was acting as though she were the one trying to convince him.

"What the hell do you mean?" she snapped with what she thought was perfectly justifiable anger. "Who's playing games now? This was your idea."

"True," he admitted. "But just like you, I've had second thoughts."

"Why?"

"Let's just say your turnaround seems a bit too sudden. I'm not convinced it's what you really want. I have a feeling you think it's something you should do, just to prove a point."

"And what point would that be?"

"That you're as liberated as Karen."

Barrie paled at the possibly accurate and distinctly uncomfortable charge but replied slowly, "I don't have to prove a damn thing to you."

"Certainly not that," he agreed. "Maybe you're trying to prove something to yourself. Why don't we get together tonight and discuss this again when we have more time?"

"You know very well that I have a taping tonight."

"Maybe I can get a ticket," he suggested dryly. Barrie could just imagine the smug, teasing glint in his blue-green eyes. The image made her go weak in the knees. If the mere thought of him could do that, it was no wonder his real-life presence had made her abandon all good sense. Good Lord, had she actually considered moving in with the impossible man? Clearly her mind had been warped by the stress of getting her first series on the air. She should have thrown herself onto the couch of a shrink, instead of into the arms of a thoroughly egotistical network executive. She should be grateful that he'd dismissed her surrender so easily.

She sighed. So why didn't she feel grateful? Why did she feel betrayed and lonely? She wasn't at all sure she wanted to know the answer to those questions. Had she been counting on living with Michael even more than she'd realized?

Despite the perversity of those feelings, she mustered her most casual tone and replied, "Give it your best shot, Compton, but I hear we're booked up."

"No problem. I'll stand backstage."

"You do, and I'll wrap an electrical cord around your neck."

"Why?" he asked innocently. "Will my presence make you nervous?"

"Of course not," she lied boldly. He was the last person on earth she wanted to see tonight, but she'd be damned if she'd admit that to him. "But we do have a rule about outsiders being backstage, and I don't intend to break it for you."

"I'm hardly an outsider," he reminded her tartly. "I'll see you tonight."

Predictably enough, considering the way the day had started, the evening turned into an absolute disaster. Michael arrived just as they discovered that too many tickets had been given out for the taping. A crowd of angry tourists was lined up outside the studio. Barrie was afraid they'd storm the door right in the middle of the show.

To top it off, once the show began, the cast performed as though they'd never had a minute's rehearsal. Melinda's timing was awful. Some of the actors were forgetting their lines, leaving the others to flounder helplessly. As a result, the studio audience was not laughing in the right places, which had Heath pacing frantically around backstage, muttering dire threats against each and every member of the cast.

When the sound system broke down, delaying the taping for over an hour, Barrie felt like abandoning the entire production and hiding in her office. Instead, torn between humiliation that Michael had been a witness to all this chaos and confusion and her very real need to have his admiration, she tried to maintain a cool, competent facade as she set out to deal with each crisis.

But before she could take control, in each instance Michael was one step ahead of her, promising the tourists tickets for another taping, calming the cast, bolstering Heath's spirits, even rolling up his sleeves and working alongside the technicians on the sound system. Barrie began to feel helpless and unnecessary. The more useless she felt, the angrier she got.

"Damn it, Compton, get off my set," she finally said in a low, measured tone that was filled with barely controlled fury. His eyes widened as he looked up at her in astonishment from his place amid the cables that crisscrossed the floor. A hush fell over the backstage area.

"What's wrong?"

"You're doing it again," she snapped.

"Doing what again?" he said blankly.

"Taking over."

"I'm just trying to help," he protested.

"I don't need your help, at least not this kind. I need you just to be nice to me, to be supportive. Can't you pretend for a few minutes that you don't know a damn thing about television? Just pat me on the head and tell me everything will be okay, that I can handle it, instead of treating me like some kind of incompetent imbecile who's incapable of dealing with stress or running her own show."

"Is that what I was doing?"

"Of course it is. The minute things started falling apart tonight, you didn't wait to see if I could manage, you just jumped right in and started giving orders."

Michael took a deep breath, his expression thoroughly abashed. "I thought I was pitching in to help, but I can see how it might not seem that way to you," he said apologetically. "I'm sorry if you thought I was being patronizing."

Barrie sighed and ran her fingers through her hair. "No," she said at last, "I'm the one who's sorry. I know you're just trying to help. I'm being overly sensitive. I didn't want you to see things unless they were perfect. And tonight was far from perfect."

"Nothing ever goes as smoothly as a producer would like it to," he consoled her.

"Maybe not," she said wryly. "But I think tonight was a bit beyond the norm."

"You could have handled it if I'd stayed out of your way."

She grinned at him impudently. "I know I could."

"From now on, if you'd prefer, I'll stay away from the tapings."

"Promise?"

He gave her his most beguiling smile, and her heart flipped over. "Well, I might just peek in occasionally...."

"Michael!"

"I won't stay. I promise. You can handle each and every crisis on your own without any interference from me. Write that on a piece of paper, and I'll sign it in blood."

The tension finally broke, and she laughed at his solemn oath. "You don't have to go that far. I trust you."

"I'm glad," he said, gathering her into his arms and holding her tightly. He whispered into her ear, "Now what was it you were saying about wanting someone's shoulder to lean on?"

"Not here," she murmured as his hands caressed her back, sending a shiver of sparks cascading down her spine.

"Why not?"

"We do have a taping to finish," she reminded him. "This delay is going to drive production costs up."

His hands fell away from her immediately. She grinned up at him. "I thought that might get to you."

"Later?" he suggested.

"Later."

It was three hours before the taping finally ended, and by then Barrie was completely drained. Michael had been true to his word and had stayed out of the way for the remainder of the taping, but, perversely, there had been times when she wished he'd ignored her earlier warning and taken charge. By ten o'clock she was awfully tired of being competent and independent.

"You all set?" Michael asked when he found her sitting on the audience bleachers staring at the set.

"Almost."

He followed the direction of her gaze. "What's wrong?"

"There was something odd about the set tonight. Melinda kept bumping into things. I can't figure it out, I'm sure this is the way it was last week."

"No, it's not."

Barrie looked at him in surprise. "It's not?"

"Nope. You've moved the sofa off-center. It looks better, but it's not as easy for her to walk around it where it is now. The aisle's too narrow, and the desk gets in the way."

He walked onto the set and nudged the sofa about two feet to the left. "That's the way it was before."

"You're amazing."

He beamed at her. "That's me."

"Remind me never to try to sneak something out of your office. You probably know down to a tenth of an inch where each piece of paper is."

"I remember the symmetry, but I don't always recall the content."

"That's reassuring. I'll just have to replace what I take with another piece of paper."

"You sound as though you're planning a burglary in the near future. Wouldn't it be easier to ask for whatever you want?"

"Not in this case."

"Why not?"

She hesitated, then finally admitted in a rush, "I want those notes you made the other day on Karen."

He chuckled. "I think I see why you didn't want to ask. Are you ready to make the changes?"

"Let's just say I'm beginning to agree that there's room for some modification. She seemed a little strident tonight. I thought Heath and I could take another look at her."

He sat on the bleacher next to her and cupped her chin in his hand. "Thank you," he said softly. "I know how hard it was for you to admit that."

"I'm not promising we'll make any changes," she countered quickly. "Just that I want to go over what you had in mind again."

"That's a start." He leaned forward and kissed her, a hungry, urgent kiss that drew her into his arms and left her wanting more as her blood roared in her veins.

"That was quite a start, too," she murmured with a sigh. She grinned at him impishly. "You're turning into quite a tease, Michael Compton."

"Me? A tease?" he squawked indignantly.

"Yes, you. First you back out on living together. Then twice in one night you start something you apparently have no intention of finishing."

"Who says?"

"Well, then?"

"You mean now? Here?"

He was examining the hard bleacher warily. "I suppose it's possible."

"Oh, I think we can do better than this. Come with me."

"But my car is here. I'll follow you."

"No way. Your car will be here in the morning. The guards wouldn't dare let anyone steal it."

"Okay," he finally agreed enthusiastically, apparently determining that the wicked gleam in her eyes could only work in his favor. "Lead on, Miss Mac-Donald. I'm all yours."

"I wish," she murmured under her breath as they got into her car.

"What's that?"

"Never mind."

Barrie had always enjoyed driving as long as she wasn't competing with a bumper-to-bumper collection of maniacs, and at this hour the road was relatively free of traffic. As she zipped west toward the beach, she and Michael chatted easily about everything but television. Despite the casual, innocuous conversation, however, she didn't let him forget for a minute that she had something far more intimate on her mind. Each time she shifted gears, she allowed her hand to caress his inner thigh or left it resting gently on his knee, her fingers seeking an interesting little erogenous zone she'd discovered along the curve of his muscle.

After one of these none-too-casual assaults, Michael moaned softly, and she glanced over to find him leaning back in his seat with his eyes closed and a satisfied smile on his lips. She took her hand away.

"Uh-uh," he protested, grabbing it and putting it back, this time a little higher where she could feel the hard surge of his arousal. Her pulse pounded. Her little game was getting out of hand. If she wasn't careful, they'd end up trying to make love in a gas station parking lot with a gear shift poking in her ribs. Somehow there was no romance in that particular image.

This time when she staged a more forceful retreat, he let her go, but she could tell from the grin tugging at his lips that he knew he'd gotten to her just as effectively as she'd stirred him. When she pulled the car to a stop and switched off the engine, he opened his eyes and peered outside.

"Where are we?"

Barrie shook her head. "For a man who only a short time ago could tell that a sofa was slightly out of place, you seem to have lost your powers of observation. That is the Pacific Ocean."

"I recognized that much."

"Well, then?"

"I suppose a more appropriate question might be: What are we doing here?"

She leaned over and brushed a tantalizing kiss across his lips, and her fingers nestled in the warm curve where thigh and hip met. "What do you think?"

Michael's eyes widened. "Here?"

"It's softer than the bleachers."

"It is also sandy."

"I have a blanket in the trunk."

"Were you planning this, or do you come here often?"

"I come here quite a bit."

"Like hell, you do," he growled.

"Alone, Compton. Alone," she said soothingly. "It's a good place to sit and think."

"Oh."

They took the blanket into a secluded cove and spread it out. While Michael stretched out, Barrie stood over him, bathed in moonlight, and slowly removed her clothes. As each item was discarded, his breathing grew increasingly ragged. When she'd tossed aside the last item, her lacy bikini panties, Michael reached for her, but she stepped just beyond his reach.

"Last one in has to fix breakfast," she taunted, racing for the water.

"Why you..." Michael sputtered as he tried to pull off his clothes while chasing after her. His pants tangled around his legs, and he fell, sprawling, into the sand. By then she was already waist deep in the water, laughing at his expression of pure frustration.

He stripped off the rest of his clothes then and stood, and suddenly the laughter died on her lips. With soft moonlight bathing him in a silvery glow, he looked like some sort of an impressive god standing on the shore, his athletic body trim, firm and very, very masculine.

"If I have to come in after you, you are in a lot of trouble, Barrie MacDonald," he warned in a low, provocative voice that sent a shiver racing through her.

"I'm not afraid of you," she retorted bravely, though with each step he took toward her, her racing pulse told her she ought to be. When he dove into the silver-highlighted darkness of the midnight sea and disappeared from view, she tried to gauge his approach to elude him. But it was impossible, and she knew it. She gasped when his hands glided up her legs, circled her waist and then brushed upward against the taut slipperiness of her already aching breasts.

Burning lips caressed hers, blazed a path over slender shoulders to the full curve of her breasts. Each sensitized tip was suckled in turn as Barrie's back arched to give him full access.

"Barrie MacDonald, I want you," he murmured in a husky growl that inflamed her, "I want to make love to you, to feel you come alive to my touch."

With great urgency and tenderness he scooped her up into his powerful arms and carried her to the blanket. Lowering her gently, he knelt poised over her, and Barrie felt a growing tension in her abdomen. Her body was ready for him, needed him. She held her arms up to him.

"Love me," she pleaded urgently. "Now."

He shook his head. "Not yet. We have all night."

His touches began then with her face. Gentle lips were followed by caressing fingers that teased and taunted until her skin seemed on fire. There was no part of her that did not receive his loving adoration, not one square inch of her flesh that had not felt the moistness of his tongue, the gentleness of his hands.

"Please," she murmured, her body arching toward him, seeking the fulfillment he withheld.

"Not yet," he whispered again, his fingers seeking, probing, delighting until she cried out with pleasure. The tension subsided with the release, but then it was building again, urged ever higher by his relentless, knowing touch. She was bathed in a sheen of perspiration that glistened in the moonlight. Michael's eyes darkened with passion as he watched her, and Barrie felt more beautiful, more desirable, more beloved than she'd ever imagined possible.

Once more the flames of passion engulfed her, and she moaned as she sought Michael's body, tried to draw him to her. This time he relented, and with a powerful surge he filled her. Their rhythmic movements were perfectly timed, creating an exquisite tension that built and built until Barrie felt a scream tear out from someplace deep inside her as the tension exploded into a thousand glittering bits. Michael held himself poised as the tremors rocked her, increasing her satisfaction. And, then, when her own pleasure was complete, he took his, his body trembling with violent shudders as his excitement peaked.

The unbearable intensity of the experience left them both breathless and seemingly speechless. They were wrapped in each other's arms, and it was a long time before Barrie finally murmured softly, plaintively, "Michael, what do you want from me? What is it you really want?"

He sighed deeply and held her tighter.

"Sweetheart, I don't have an answer to that," he confessed honestly. "At least not the definitive kind you're looking for. I know that I need you, that I care about you. You've brought something into my life that I hadn't even known I was missing. I just know that now that I've found it, I can't do without it. You are so special to me. You're warm and intelligent and feisty. You're incredibly sexy. Yet there's a vulnerability about you that makes me want to protect you. I want you with me, where I can keep an eye on you. I need you.''

Want. Need. Barrie listened to Michael's words, tried to hear what he wasn't saying, as much as what he was. As much as she yearned to hear it, he wasn't saying he was in love with her. A couple of months ago that wouldn't have mattered to her. Moments such as those they had just shared would have been more than enough.

With each day that had passed, however, she had fallen more deeply, more hopelessly in love with him. Admitting that finally had been such a relief. Overcoming all those years of fearing heartbreak hadn't been easy. In fact, she doubted that a lesser man than Michael could have brought her to this point, and she was grateful to him for forcing her out of her emotional hiding place.

But now she desperately wanted his love in return. She sighed and curved her body into his, listening to the reassuring beat of his heart. Surely a love to match hers was there. He had only to find it.

Now she was the one who would have to wait patiently. And hope.

Eleven

A week later, Barrie and Michael were sitting across from each other at her desk, eating the take-out Chinese food he had brought over for lunch, when the phone rang. She wrinkled her nose in disgust at the intrusion.

"Not again," she moaned. "You're going to eat every bit of this fried rice before I get my first grain, if this blasted phone doesn't calm down."

"You could ignore it," he suggested, scooping more rice out of the container with exaggerated glee. "You know it's not your boss or your lover."

"Who says?" she countered wickedly as she picked up the phone and said in a pointedly low, seductive tone, "Barrie MacDonald."

"Hey, sweetheart, how've you been?"

She immediately recognized the voice of Jeff Taylor, a sweet, intelligent attorney with whom she'd spent several pleasant but unexciting evenings. She grinned to herself. Perfect. She would teach Michael Compton a thing or two about smug overconfidence!

"Jeff, sweetheart, how are you?" she said enthusiastically, noting that Michael's brows lifted quizzically, and his interest in the conversation seemed to pick up dramatically at the mention of a male's name. His chopsticks were poised midway to his mouth, and the shrimp and rice were dribbling back unnoticed onto his plate. She practically groaned out loud. Men! What predictable, territorial creatures they were.

"I'm terrific. I've been away on business for the past month."

"Really. Anyplace interesting?"

"Hawaii. One of my clients was having some problems with his properties over there."

"Nice work, if you can get it. I wouldn't mind being sent to Hawaii on business," she said, looking pointedly at Michael. He made a face at her.

"Now that I'm back, I thought maybe we could get together. I have tickets for a play tomorrow night. Are you free?"

Barrie had expected such an invitation from the moment she recognized Jeff's voice. She'd certainly known that he wasn't calling to chat about the weather or his trip to Hawaii. Still, she had no idea how to answer him. Certainly she was free enough. Michael hadn't made any plans with her for tomorrow or the rest of the weekend. He rarely planned much in advance for their evenings together, seeming to take it for granted that she would be available. Nor had they made any commitments to see each other exclusively since their disastrous discussion about living together.

So why was she hesitating? Only because he was sitting right there in front of her? No. She'd be torn by indecision even if he were well out of sight.

Common sense told her there was absolutely no reason to turn down a date with another attractive man. Her gut told her she'd have a lousy time and that she'd spend the whole evening comparing Jeff with Michael, to the attorney's tremendous disadvantage. Common sense and his current reaction to a mere phone call told her it might do Michael even more good to realize he was not the only man in her life interested in taking her out. Her gut told her it would be a game, and it was childish to start playing it now.

"Barrie? Are you still there?"

"Sorry. I'm here, Jeff. I was just checking my calendar." She flipped the page over and looked at the vast emptiness on Saturday and Sunday.

Michael was no longer even making a pretense of eating, and he was scowling at her with an expression that would have kept even Romeo and Juliet apart. She ignored him and debated her response.

"And?" Jeff said hopefully. "Don't say no, Barrie. I've really missed you."

The sincerity in his voice, more than anything else, clinched it. It would hardly be fair to go out with a man who'd just admitted to missing her, when she hadn't given him a thought since their last date over a month ago.

"I wish I could go, Jeff, but I'm busy," she said at last. To her amazement, Michael breathed what sounded like a sigh of relief at her polite rejection.

"Another time, then."

"Sure. Another time," she said, knowing that that time would never come. "You take care, Jeff. It was good to hear from you."

"Who was that?" Michael growled before she could even put the receiver back into place.

"A friend."

"Were you serious about him?"

"Why do you put that in the past tense?"

"Because I assume you're no longer serious about him."

"Don't assume anything, Mr. Compton," she taunted. "It makes one too complacent."

"Very cute," he muttered as he glanced at his watch and jumped to his feet. "I'm late."

So much for concern about his competition. It seemed to have vanished in a puff of renewed self-confidence. Barrie glared at him and wished she'd kept him dangling a little longer. She sighed. It was too late now. He had already surmised that the faceless Jeff was not important in her life.

"See you later," he announced casually.

"Oh, really?" she asked innocently, hoping to stir some new doubts. The man was definitely getting to be too sure of himself. She glanced pointedly down at the blank page of her calendar again. "Did we have plans?"

"We do now," he said, kissing her thoroughly before rushing out the door. On his way out he practically crashed into Heath and Danielle, who were so embroiled in yet another heated argument about the latest script for *Goodbye, Again* that they barely acknowledged him.

"What's the problem this time?" Barrie asked them resignedly, picking hungrily at the little mound of fried rice not ravaged by Michael.

"I say Karen should go out with another man, even though she's involved with Mason," Heath explained.

Barrie's head jerked up as she was struck by the strangest sense of déjà vu. The show was mirroring her life again.

"I mean, why not?" Heath continued, glowering at Danielle. "There's no commitment. She hadn't made any promises to him, and this other guy is pursuing her."

"Is she attracted to him?" Barrie asked curiously, wondering if her lack of interest in Jeff Taylor physically had played a role in her refusal of his invitation.

"The guy is a hunk. Of course she's attracted to him. That's what it's all about."

"But is that kind of attraction alone enough for her to risk hurting Mason?" Danielle demanded skeptically. "I don't think so. It makes her seem shallow and callous."

"No. It just shows she has a strong sense of her own sexual needs. She'd think Mason could—or should—take it, just the way women have been accepting it for years that unless they're married to a guy, he's got the right to roam."

Danielle turned to Barrie for support. "What do you think?"

"I don't know," Barrie admitted finally. "A month ago I'd have said let her go. Mason can stand up for himself. But now it seems wrong." Just as it had seemed wrong to her only moments ago to accept a date with Jeff Taylor simply to make Michael jealous. She appealed to Danielle, tears glistening in her eyes. "What's happening to me?"

Danielle's face was instantly full of concern. "Sweetie, it's just a television show. Why are you so upset?"

Before she could explain, she realized that Heath was staring at her as though she'd betrayed him. "I thought you were the liberated woman, just like Karen. What's good for the goose is good for the gander, and all that sort of thing."

"Your sense of timing is lousy, Donaldson," Danielle growled. "Can't you see that? Get out of here."

"But we haven't settled this."

"We'll settle it later."

When he had gone, Barrie admitted to Danielle that her own emotional turmoil was forcing her to rethink the character she'd created, as well. The Karen she'd created wouldn't have thought twice about dating a whole string of men, even if one of them happened to care very deeply for her and she for him. There would have been emotional safety in a crowd, protection from a commitment that could go painfully awry.

"But I can't play it safe that way anymore," she confessed. "It wouldn't do any good, anyway. I'm in love with Michael."

Danielle raised her hands in a victory gesture. "At last," she said triumphantly. "Are you going to marry him?"

Barrie quirked a brow. "Who said anything about marriage? He won't even live with me, and he's certainly not in love with me."

"Oh, posh-tosh. Who says?"

"I do. I practically asked him point-blank, and he avoided using those words as if they were missing from his vocabulary. He said everything else but that. He cares. He wants me. He needs me. But love? Forget it."

"Honey, I've seen the look in that man's eyes. He's not about to let you get away, and I don't think he'll settle for anything less than marriage, no matter what he does or doesn't say. Give him some time." She grinned at Barrie. "Don't you think those incredible thighs are worth waiting for?"

"I'm more interested in his mind."

"Uh-huh. Of course you are," Danielle said dryly.

"A man's legs are not a great basis for a marriage."

"Maybe," Danielle retorted without conviction. "Think of it this way, then. You'll never have to explain to him what a demographic is or how a rating is determined, *and* he has great thighs. Where would you ever find another man with those credentials?"

Barrie winced. "Don't even mention ratings. Every time I look at ours, I get this sick feeling in the pit of my stomach."

"They'll get better."

"And if they don't?"

"If they don't, you can just remind yourself that it was *Goodbye, Again* that brought you and Michael together."

"It may be the thing that drives us apart, too," she countered candidly.

"I love your optimism."

"I'm just trying to be realistic."

"The reality is that Michael Compton is crazy about you, and I refuse to listen to any more of your silly doubts."

"I thought that's what I paid you for."

"No. You pay me to direct a television show. Being your friend is something I do out of the goodness of my heart and because of my insatiable curiosity."

"Curiosity?"

"Of course. Ever since I realized you intended to set the world on its ear, I've wanted to stick around and see how it turned out."

"How am I doing so far?"

"You're getting better every day. Now plan something spectacular for tonight, something dear old Michael won't be able to resist."

"Any idea what that might be?"

Danielle feigned shock. "My dear, I don't know the man *that* well." She winked at her. "But you sure do."

When Danielle had gone, Barrie tried to think of something wildly romantic and impetuous that would set Michael Compton on his ear. She ticked off every fantasy she'd ever had, every tale she'd heard of other crazy, funfilled flings. When the perfect idea finally struck her, she couldn't wait to put her plan into action. She made several phone calls, had a hurried conference with Danielle about that night's taping, then raced out of the studio to take care of several errands. At four-thirty she walked into Michael's office unannounced.

His head was bent over the papers on his desk, and a frown of concentration knit his brows. He was so engrossed in his work, that he didn't even glance up at her entrance. She cleared her throat loudly.

"Just put them over there," he muttered without looking up.

"Put what over where?"

His head came up then, and he stared at her in surprise. A slow, sensual smile transformed his face. Barrie smiled back. So far, so good. He hadn't tossed her out on her ear.

"Busy?" she asked, perching on the edge of his desk.

"Not too busy to see you. What's up? Has something happened since I saw you at lunch?"

"Can you take a break?"

He dropped his pencil and leaned back. "Sure. I'm all yours."

"Good. Come with me."

He shook his head. "I said I could take a break. I didn't mean I could get away from the office."

"Sure you can," Barrie countered confidently.

"I have appointments yet this afternoon."

"Not anymore."

He stared at her blankly. "What do you mean?"

"I mean they've been cancelled."

"Who cancelled them?"

"I did."

His expression altered to one of shocked disbelief. "Barrie, how could you do that? They were important."

"Not as important as what I have in mind. I checked with Mrs. Hastings just to be sure," she said firmly. "Now get your jacket and come on."

He sighed and relented finally. "When you get that determined little gleam in your eye, I suppose it's pointless for me to refuse."

"Do you really want to?"

He looked from her to Mrs. Hastings, who was standing in the doorway beaming at the two of them with maternalistic satisfaction.

"You're involved in this conspiracy, aren't you? You know what's going on?" he demanded of her.

"Yes, sir," she replied dutifully.

"Would you mind telling me?"

She grinned at Barrie, then looked back at him with an expression of pure innocence. "Sorry. I've been sworn to secrecy."

"But you're my secretary," he reminded her, then added pointedly, "For now."

"I am also a woman who loves surprises," she retorted tartly. "And don't you go threatening me, young man. I was here before you came, and I daresay I'll be here after you're gone. Now you just run along and have a good time. Don't be such a stuffed shirt."

"Stuffed shirt?" Michael's eyes widened, and he shot Barrie an accusing glance. "Are you proud of yourself? It's your fault that my secretary called me a stuffed shirt."

"And well she should," Barrie commented dryly. "I've never seen a grown man so terrified of a little surprise."

"The last time someone tried to surprise me I walked into a room filled with 300 of my nearest and dearest friends, all of whom had been celebrating so long before my arrival that they barely noticed me."

"That must have been a blow to your ego," Barrie commented, grinning at him.

"If it will help, I guarantee you that I'll notice you," she promised seductively. "In fact, I won't take my eyes off you."

He threw up his hands in a gesture of surrender. "Okay. When you put it like that, I don't dare refuse. Lead on."

Outside, Michael's limousine was waiting with the driver standing smartly at attention.

"What's he doing here?"

"It's part of the surprise."

"You ordered my limousine?"

Barrie shook her head. "Of course not," she denied indignantly. "Mrs. Hastings did."

"Thank goodness," he chuckled. "I see. Is there any point in my asking where we're going?"

"None."

"I don't like this," he said as they entered the limo.

"You don't like not being in control. Relax."

"I'm virtually kidnapped out of my own office in the middle of the afternoon, and you tell me to relax. You're the kidnapper. Why should I trust you?"

"Because I'm entirely trustworthy."

"That remains to be seen."

Barrie reached into her purse and extracted a white scarf. Michael eyed her doubtfully.

"What's that?"

"A scarf."

"I know that. What's it for?"

Barrie took a deep breath. This was going to be the hard part. She groaned. Who was she kidding? It might very well be the impossible part.

"It's a blindfold," she offered casually.

Before she'd completed the sentence, Michael was already shaking his head. Decisively. "Uh-uh. No way. I draw the line at blindfolds."

"Michael," she said sweetly, curving herself into his side and running her fingers down his chest. She could feel his heartbeat speed up. "Remember how much fun we had when you talked me into getting onto the swing?"

He eyed her warily. "What does that have to do with anything?"

"Remember how pleased you were that I was willing to take a risk on that?"

"Yes," he said slowly, his eyes narrowing distrustfully. "But I am not wearing that blindfold," he repeated adamantly.

Barrie stared directly into his eyes and waited. Their gazes locked, held. "Please."

Michael moaned. "Barrie," he pleaded.

"Michael." Her tone was soft, cajoling.

"Oh, okay. Give me the damn thing."

She smiled at him brightly. "Thank you."

As soon as the blindfold was in place, she reached back into her purse. "Now, hold still a minute."

"What the hell are you doing now?"

"Ear plugs."

"What!" Michael's shout reverberated through the limousine, and Barrie noted that the driver's glance in the rearview mirror was thoroughly amused. "Forget it!"

"Please, Michael. Don't spoil my surprise."

"Dear Lord, woman, what are you up to?"

"It's just for a little while. I promise."

When the earplugs were in place, Barrie sat back in satisfaction and held tightly onto Michael's hand. Her grip was intended to keep him from ripping off the blindfold and tearing out the earplugs even more than it was to feel the warmth of his touch. She had a feeling his compliance with her odd demands would be very short-lived. Fortunately she only needed another half hour or so.

They completed the ride in silence, and when the car stopped, Michael immediately reached for the blindfold with his free hand. Barrie nabbed his hand in the nick of time and removed one ear plug.

"Not yet," she said and quickly put the plug back in place.

With the assistance of the driver, she led Michael from the car, across the pavement and up a long flight of stairs, ignoring his angry mutterings and the amused grins of everyone they passed. When they reached their destination, she pushed him down into a seat, thanked the driver and sat down next to him. By now he was thoroughly docile, though she had a feeling that at any minute he would rise up and rebel.

When she heard the engines roar to life, she breathed a sigh of relief.

And when the plane began taxiing down the runway, she reached over and removed the ear plugs and blindfold.

"Where the hell are we?" Michael immediately grumbled, looking around. His eyebrows shot up in amazement. "We're on a plane."

He couldn't have looked any more stunned if he'd found himself on a spaceship. "What are we doing on a plane?"

"Going to dinner," she announced casually, picking up a magazine and thumbing through it. He snatched it from her.

"Look me in the eye and say that again."

"We're going to dinner," she repeated, staring him straight in the eye.

"Where?" He sounded shaky.

"Hawaii."

Once the full impact of what Barrie had done sank in, Michael burst out laughing, much to her relief.

"You're incredible!" he announced, giving her a kiss that literally took her breath away.

She regarded him closely. He seemed happy enough. "You're not angry?"

"How can I be mad at a beautiful woman who is taking me to dinner in one of the most romantic places in the world?" He paused. "You are taking me, aren't you? Or is part of the surprise that I'm paying for all of this?"

She grinned at him impishly. "Well, Mrs. Hastings did make the arrangements. She was sure you were too much of a gentleman to let me pay."

"Right," he said dryly.

"I did offer."

"I'm sure you did. Mrs. Hastings is a very generous woman...with my money." He reached up and pushed the call light for the stewardess. "I think I could use a drink."

Barrie watched him warily. The last thing she'd wanted to do was get the sweet, very cooperative Mrs. Hastings into trouble. "Don't be mad at her," she begged. "After all, this was my idea."

"I know that," he said. "She'd never dream this one up on her own."

"You're not going to fire her, are you?"

"Good heavens, no. Didn't you hear her say she'd be around the network long after I was gone? She knows where all the bodies are buried. She could blackmail every one of us."

"Mrs. Hastings would never do that!" Barrie replied indignantly. "She is the kindest, sweetest, most loyal secretary in the world. She adores you."

"Don't you ever tell her, but I think she's pretty terrific, too. Though I think I'll remind her that the next time some liberated woman wants to fly me across the Pacific for dinner, she should keep my credit card numbers out of it."

"If we talk about the show, you could charge it to your expense account," Barrie suggested slyly. "Would you feel better about that?"

Michael's eyes widened. "My God! The show! It's Friday. You have a taping tonight."

"Don't worry about it. Danielle's handling everything. The rehearsal came off last night without a hitch. Tonight will be a breeze."

"What happened to that noble producer who kept telling me that she was part of a team and that she'd never abandon them?"

"I'm not abandoning them. I'm letting them try out their wings. Everyone can use a little independence, you know," she told him nonchalantly.

"Are you sure Heath won't rewrite the script and put in a passionate love scene just to get even with us for leaving?"

"If he does, we can just edit it out again," she soothed. "Now stop worrying."

He chuckled suddenly. "It's nice to see you finally loosening up."

"What is that supposed to mean?"

"That the woman I met a few weeks ago would never have walked away from her television show for a mere dinner date."

"Love, this is no *mere dinner date*, as you call it," she retorted, adding with dramatic emphasis, "We are having a romantic fling."

His smile widened, and he put his arm around her. "Tell me more," he murmured softly into her ear. "This is sounding better and better."

Twelve

Dinner on the terrace of a suite overlooking the ocean and Diamond Head had been sheer perfection. Soft breezes filled with sweet tropical scents touched their skin with a lover's gentleness, and the swaying of palm trees created an island music. A basket of fresh Hawaiian fruit, a bottle of chilled champagne and orchids on the pillows had provided the romantic finishing touches. But it was Michael's tenderness, his exquisite caresses, his whispered words that had filled the evening with romance.

Barrie lay by his side at dawn and watched him, her body sated, her heart filled to overflowing with a love more powerful than she had ever dared to dream of. She had hardly slept, not wanting to miss a moment of this beautiful time together. She couldn't seem to get enough of the sheer joy of looking at him, at his broad chest with its masculine shadow of hair, at his flat stomach, his curved bottom and those thick muscular thighs that seemed to symbolize exactly how powerful and virile he was.

As she stared at his sleeping form, a smile tilted his lips, and she sensed a stirring beneath the sheet that lay provocatively draped across his hips. She ran her finger down his chest and heard a low moan rumble in his chest as he rolled into her touch, his body, hot and urgent against hers. Stirred to excitement yet again by no more than that, she was ready for him, her hands playing over his body, urging him back to a complete wakefulness and a shattering climax for both of them.

"Sorry," he murmured sleepily against her ear as he cradled her in his arms.

She pulled back and stared into his eyes. "Sorry for what?"

"That couldn't have been very good for you. I was half asleep."

"Everything you do is good for me," she corrected him. "And if you were so sleepy, how do I know you didn't miss the best parts?"

He chuckled. "And what might those have been?"

"This," she said, her lips brushing across his shoulder and trailing a line of fire down his chest until her tongue dipped into the indentation of his navel.

"And this," she murmured, her fingers dancing across his abdomen, capturing the heart of his masculinity, which was ready again. "You know, Mr. Compton, you're pretty amazing."

"Only with you sweetheart. Only with you."

"I hope that's true," she said, unable to keep a note of wistfulness out of her voice.

He looked at her closely. "Do you doubt it?"

She remembered all the advice she'd ever read about not admitting to doubts. And she recalled yet more sage counsel that honesty in a relationship was the best policy. She opted for honesty. "Sometimes, yes."

"Don't ever doubt it," he soothed, cupping her face and forcing her to meet his eyes. "I may not know how to say it right, but you are the first woman I've ever cared about this way. The feelings we share are completely unique in my experience, and I don't ever want to lose that."

"You won't have to," Barrie said, her heart suddenly lighter and filled with song. A love song. They might not have been a proposal or even an obvious declaration of love, but his words contained a powerful commitment nonetheless, and she rejoiced in what he had said.

He brushed a kiss across her lips. "I'm glad to see the smile back." He stacked the pillows at the head of the bed and pulled himself into a sitting position, then settled Barrie in his arms.

"Now tell me something."

"What?"

"Now that we've had dinner...and breakfast, is there more to this surprise of yours?"

Barrie's brow creased in a tiny frown. "I never thought beyond last night," she admitted. "Isn't that ridiculous? I guess I just assumed we'd have to fly back this morning."

"Don't you think that would be a terrible waste of such a lovely room and idyllic setting?" he asked, running a hand across her stomach until the muscles in her abdomen contracted with an unbearable tension. When his fingers touched her sensitive breasts, Barrie gasped.

"Now that you mention it," she replied breathlessly.

"What shall we do about it, then?"

"I think you're on the right track."

"I thought so too," he admitted with a grin, as he intensified his touches until Barrie was writhing with pleasure and welcoming him back inside her.

For the next twenty-four hours they never left the room, sleeping only when they were so exhausted they could no longer talk or make love, ordering room service in the middle of the night when fresh pineapple and flat champagne were no longer enough to sustain them. Barrie knew that if she lived to be one hundred she would never again meet anyone who could bring her such joy, who could satisfy her so completely on so many levels. And when, just as she fell asleep, she thought she heard Michael murmur that he loved her, she was sure her heart would explode with happiness.

When they returned to Los Angeles late Sunday night, she was also certain that they were committed at last and that it would only be a matter of time before Michael said those three vital words aloud in broad daylight and followed them with a marriage proposal she knew she would accept. She had absolutely no fears any more about the future or about their ability to sustain their love for a lifetime. Michael had given her freedom from the past.

But as the next few weeks flew by, that incredible feeling of a perfect harmony with her mate was tempered by her concern over *Goodbye, Again*. She grew to dread the beginning of each new week, when the national ratings were announced. *Goodbye, Again* had crept up a bit its second week on the air but then slid right back down to the bottom. The cast and crew were demoralized, and there didn't seem to be a thing she could do. Pep talks were no longer nearly enough. Although she knew that Michael had been right about the show's tone, that had been fixed, and she was certain now that the real problem was that horrible Saturday night time slot over which she had absolutely no control.

"Dani, I don't know what to do. I feel so helpless," she said late one Tuesday afternoon after looking at the latest ratings. "I've tried talking to Michael about it, but it's getting more and more awkward."

"When do you try talking to him?"

Barrie looked at her oddly. "What do you mean? I talk to him whenever I get the chance."

"Like late at night? In bed?"

She began to see where Danielle was headed. "Okay. Yes. I suppose that's not the best place."

"That's the understatement of the year. You're the one who's been saying all along that having a business and personal relationship confuses things. Maybe you should try separating them again. Make an appointment and talk to the man in his office. That's where he makes his business decisions."

Barrie grinned at her. "And here I'd always heard the president got some of his best advice for running the country at home in bed."

"Maybe so, but the first lady is on his side. In the case of *Goodbye, Again*, you and Michael may be members of opposition parties."

Danielle was right, and Barrie reluctantly admitted it to her. "Okay, you win. I'll call over there right now and see what his calendar looks like for this afternoon."

Unfortunately, according to Mrs. Hastings, Michael's calendar looked crammed for the next week.

"He's flying to New York this afternoon, and I'm not sure when he'll be back."

"He's going this afternoon?" Barrie said incredulously. "He never mentioned a trip. Was it sudden?"

"No, dear. I don't think so. I made the arrangements several days ago."

"Oh," Barrie's voice was flat. "Well, never mind, Mrs. Hastings. "I'll set up something when he gets back."

"That will be fine, dear," she replied, then added kindly, "Don't be upset about his trip. I'm sure he meant to tell you. He's been terribly busy and distracted lately."

"Sure," Barrie agreed without conviction. "Thanks."

"What's wrong?" Danielle asked the minute the receiver was back in place.

"He's leaving town this afternoon, and he never said one word to me about it."

"Maybe it slipped his mind."

"Dani, the man has been at my house practically every night for the past month. Surely he could have found a minute to mention that he had to go to New York. Was he just planning on not showing up tonight and calling from the East Coast later to announce, 'Oh, by the way, I won't be over later. I'm 3,000 miles away'?"

"Barrie," Danielle said warningly.

"Barrie what?"

"You're working yourself into a snit over nothing."

"Nothing?"

"At this moment, it is nothing. Give the man a chance."

"You're awfully generous. Aren't you supposed to be on my side in this?"

"I am. That's why I'm trying to get you to calm down before you blow up and say something you'll regret."

"I won't regret it when I give him a piece of my mind."

"Wanna bet?"

"I never indulge in useless regrets," she replied stoutly.

"You'd be better off if you didn't indulge that sharp tongue of yours."

"Thank you very much."

"You're welcome."

Michael did call from the airport to let Barrie know he was on his way out of town. And she did keep her mouth clamped firmly shut except to say goodbye and wish him a pleasant trip, but she didn't like it. As she told Danielle later, "I'd have felt a whole lot better if I'd let him have it."

The next morning, when she picked up the trade papers on her way into the studio, she was even sorrier that she'd restrained herself. The headline on page one of both papers referred to the cancellation of several fall television shows. Prominently mentioned in each story was the "promising comedy" *Goodbye, Again*.

"Despite being a personal favorite of network VP Michael Compton, this show suffered from anemic ratings from the start," one writer noted. "Not even his bias could save it in the end."

Barrie read the articles with her fists clenched. By the time she'd finished, she was gritting her teeth. If Michael had been in his office across the parking lot, she would have marched over there and punched him squarely in that sexy, dimpled jaw of his. How dare he! How could he make love to her night after night and then have the audacity, the absolute gall to publicly cancel her television series without saying a single word to her personally? She'd had to read it in the damned paper. No wonder the man had gone to New York. He'd wanted to be far out of her reach when she exploded.

She began muttering under her breath in graphic detail precisely what she planned to do to him when she got her hands on him. Mincemeat. That's what she'd make of him. He, not she, might have earned a reputation as someone who'd casually dissect his enemies without a second thought. But when she got through with him he'd look more innocent than Tom

Sawyer by comparison. She was not about to let him make a fool of her and get away with it. She'd have his hide first! She picked up a lovely cloisonné paperweight he'd given her and threw it across the room for emphasis. It crashed against the door, just as Danielle opened it and peeped in.

"I take it you've seen the stories."

"You bet I've seen the stories," Barrie thundered, following up with a ten minute spiel of obscenities that would have made a sailor pale. Danielle winced but came in and sat down cross-legged on the sofa to wait her out. She finally sputtered to a halt.

"Finished?" she asked cheerfully.

"Not by a long shot. That man is an arrogant, selfish, cruel son..." She started all over again.

"You're going to have a stroke if you don't calm down," Danielle observed casually at last, only barely interrupting the flow of furious words.

"Besides," she noted, "you're wasting all the good stuff on me. If you have to use such foul language, save it for Michael."

Suddenly tears filled Barrie's eyes, and she buried her head on her desk. "How could he?" she mumbled brokenly. "Dani, how could he do this without even telling me himself? Good Lord, I thought he loved me."

"Sweetie, maybe that was the problem."

"What do you mean?"

"He knew what this would do to you. Maybe he couldn't bring himself to tell you in person."

"Michael's not a coward."

"He's not cruel either, is he?"

"I never thought so before," she sniffed, hating herself for breaking down.

"Then there must be some explanation."

"There isn't an explanation in the world good enough. Michael could talk from now until hell freezes over, and I will never accept this as anything other than the worst possible kind of betrayal."

When the phone rang on her desk, she flatly refused to pick it up.

"What if it's Michael?" Danielle argued.

"Let him put whatever he has to say in a memo. He seems to enjoy that."

"You're not being very professional."

"I'm not feeling very professional. I'm feeling like a woman who's been stabbed in the back by the man she loves."

The shrill ringing finally stopped, only to start again. "I can't stand it," Danielle said with a shudder, jumping up and snatching the phone off the hook. "Barrie MacDonald's office."

Though Barrie wanted to pretend disinterest, she couldn't help listening to see if it was, in fact, Michael.

"Yes, she's in, but she's not available just now," Danielle said coolly. "No, Michael. I'm not sure when she'll be available."

Danielle was quiet for several minutes, then said at last, "How do you think she feels? She's miserable."

She nodded. "Okay, I'll tell her, but I don't think she'll listen. Bye."

"Tell me what."

"That he's sorry. That there's an explanation. That he loves you. I think that covers all of the major points."

"Right," Barrie retorted sarcastically.

"He's calling back in five minutes, and he expects to talk to you."

"I won't talk to him."

"You might as well talk to him and get it over with. I have a feeling he's not giving up."

"And exactly what is he going to do to make me listen to him when he's 3,000 miles away."

"Okay. So he can't very well tie you down long distance, but you're only postponing the inevitable. He'll be back sooner or later."

When the phone rang again, Barrie glared at it. Resignedly Danielle picked it up.

"Nope. She's still not talking." She watched Barrie as she listened. "He says you're a coward if you don't get on the line."

Barrie yanked the receiver out of Danielle's hand. "Who the hell do you think you're calling a coward?" she demanded. "I'd say you have the market cornered on that. To think that I trusted you."

"Barrie, what can I say? I'm sorry," he began apologetically. "I wanted to tell you myself, but the word leaked out yesterday before I had a chance. We weren't planning to make the announcement until next week when we'd firmed up the replacement shows."

"Were you planning on calling from New York, or were you going to send a telegram?"

"I was going to tell you in person the minute I got back. I would never handle a cancellation this way, no matter who the producer was, and I certainly wouldn't have done this to you, if I'd had any choice in the matter."

"Oh, you had a choice all right. You just made the wrong one, and now you're trying to weasel out of it."

"That's ridiculous. I love you. I would never intentionally set out to hurt you."

Barrie didn't know whether to laugh or cry. How she had longed to hear him say that he loved her. Now he was saying it in practically every other sentence, and she didn't believe him for a minute.

"Your timing is lousy, Compton. You never did understand how to write comedy."

"I'm not trying to be funny. I want to marry you."

"That's ludicrous. You've just destroyed my career. If you think I'd marry you after that, you're crazy. Marriage is no substitute for a career. A career won't betray you the way you betrayed me."

"I've hardly destroyed your career, I never meant to betray you, and I am definitely not offering marriage as a substitute. I'm proposing because I love you and I think you love me. Don't be stubborn and throw away our chance for happiness."

"Forget it," she snapped. "But I must say that line's really not too bad. Save it for you next melodrama."

"Barrie..."

She cut in curtly. "How long do we have?"

"Barrie, listen to me, please."

"How long?" she repeated adamantly.

Michael sighed wearily. "You are officially out of production now."

Barrie felt the sharp sting of tears in her eyes. "Fine. I'll be out of my office by the end of the day."

"You know that's not necessary."

"Yes," she said firmly. "It is. Goodbye, Michael."

"Barrie, wait. Please."

"Goodbye . . . Again."

Thirteen

As soon as Barrie slammed the receiver emphatically back into place, she looked at Danielle and said abruptly, "Call everyone together. I might as well get this over with."

"Are you sure you want to talk to them now while you're this upset?"

Barrie's expression was tight-lipped, but her voice was perfectly controlled. "I don't want to do it at all, but I owe it to them. I can't just sit here and sulk all day. Come back and get me as soon as everyone's here."

Danielle nodded. "Okay, sweetie. Whatever you say."

Her voice had been quietly sympathetic. Too sympathetic. As soon as she had gone, Barrie's facade of bravado slipped and she blinked away a fresh cascade of tears. Hearing Michael's voice on the phone and listening to him declare his love and ask her to marry him had ripped her apart inside. She had expected those long-desired words to be almost magical when they were finally spoken and to bring her lasting happiness. Instead she felt only empty, alone and utterly devastated.

The cancellation would have been bad enough. At least the ratings had foreshadowed that for weeks now, and she had been almost ready for it. But nothing could have prepared her for the devastation of hearing about it secondhand. Michael had obviously made the decision days ago, and surely he had owed it to her to give her some warning. No matter what sort of fluke had allowed the word to leak out prematurely, Michael should have told her himself the moment he knew there was a risk of it appearing in print.

She sighed. Well, it was too late now. As soon as she had spoken with the cast and crew, she would gather her things and leave. With any luck she would be moved out of her office long before Michael even returned to Los Angeles.

When Danielle finally tapped on her door, Barrie took a deep breath and walked back to the set with her. From the long faces and red-rimmed eyes, she could tell that they were all taking the news as hard as she had, though for very different reasons. They had not just lost a series but had also lost their jobs. She had lost all that and her lover, too. All in all it had been one hell of a morning.

She stood before them, determined not to let them see the extent of her own private pain. She clenched her hands together behind her back and fought to keep her voice under control.

"I asked Dani to gather you all together for a few minutes so I could tell you personally how proud I am of each and every one of you," she said, as Melinda sniffed and tears rolled unchecked down the cheeks of several others. Even Dani, who had remained calm for her sake earlier, was now misty-eyed. Barrie's voice almost broke, but she quickly regained her composure and spoke from her heart.

"We tried to do something special with *Goodbye, Again* and I think we accomplished what we set out to do. I'm only sorry that more people didn't see it, that the network didn't give us a chance to prove ourselves.

"I don't want any of you to regard this as a failure. Creatively, *Goodbye, Again* was the very best it could be, and your individual contributions made it that way. As you all know, this series was very special to me, and I will miss working on it. I will miss working with each of you."

She tried a wobbly smile. "But you all know television by now. We may be back together in a few months with something else even more exciting and challenging. I hope so. But whatever happens, I know that you all will go on to do great things. You're much too talented not to."

Her voice broke then and, despite her most valiant efforts, tears streamed down her face. "Thank you. I love you," she managed at last and then turned and walked briskly away. Someone started to clap behind her, and then they were all clapping. The swell of sound followed her as she went, sobbing, into her office and closed the door.

The memory of that moment of heartfelt love and support sustained her for the next few days as she sat in her apartment or walked alone on the beach to try to decide what she wanted to do next. Although her answering service had given her message after message from Michael, she had ignored them all. There was nothing he could say now that could possibly make a difference.

Only Dani had been allowed to disrupt her self-imposed isolation, and Barrie nearly regretted it each time she allowed her to visit. Not that she could have stopped her. Once Danielle started on a crusade, it would be like trying to halt a runaway freight train. Now her friend had the uncomfortable habit of bringing Michael's name into every conversation, ignoring her pleas to pretend that the man had disappeared off the face of the earth.

"He hasn't gone anywhere," Danielle retorted. "He is very much alive and, unless I miss my guess, very much in love with you."

"He had a charming way of showing it."

"The man made a mistake."

"I'll say."

"Barrie, you know what they say about forgiveness."

"That it's divine? I'm not feeling very divine right now. How can you even suggest that I just pretend this never happened?'' she demanded. "The man ruined my life."

Danielle picked up a stack of messages, most of them from network officials and other producers, all seeking a meeting with her to talk over new projects. "It doesn't appear to me that your life is ruined. There are probably a dozen solid offers waiting for you right now. You told the cast they had a future in this business. So do you."

"I'm not interested."

"What are you interested in then? You're not eating. You're not sleeping. You're not even seeing anyone but me...."

"Which I occasionally regret."

"Go ahead. Be rotten. But I'm not leaving you to work through this alone. I'm going to stay right here nudging you until you decide to get on with your life."

Barrie threw up her hands. "You are impossible."

"I am your friend. Now tell me, what are you interested in?"

"I'm thinking about moving to Des Moines and opening a dress shop. I think that's about as much excitement as my psyche can handle from now on."

Danielle nodded wisely. "That certainly makes a lot of sense. You hate cold weather. You've never been to Des Moines, and you have absolutely no idea how to run a business."

"If I can bring a television show in on schedule and under budget, surely I can pick out a few nice dresses, hang them on racks and sell them."

"And be bored to tears in the process."

Barrie gave her a smug grin. "Not when I am married to the man of my dreams."

"Oh? Is there something you haven't mentioned to me? Is Michael retiring to Des Moines, as well?"

"No. But surely there's some nice, quiet, sane man who'd be willing to take me on. I was thinking along the lines of the strong, silent type. Maybe a history professor who wears tweed jackets with those nice suede patches on the sleeves. It would be wonderful if he smoked a pipe. They smell good."

"Ah, I can see it now. Long evenings in front of the fire, watching nature shows on educational television. Long walks in the snow."

"No snow," Barrie said adamantly. "I hate snow."

"Then you'd better rethink your plan and move to Phoenix. Unless you plan to spend several months of the year indoors."

"Okay, okay," Barrie grumbled. "So Des Moines is a lousy idea, but I want something like that. I can't take any more of this glitzy roller-coaster existence out here."

"Sweetie, you thrive on this roller-coaster existence. You couldn't wait to get your first show so you could climb on."

"And now I've had it, and the ride was not all it was cracked up to be."

"The ride was exactly what you knew it would be," Danielle corrected her. "Bumpy, but exhilarating. Michael Compton is the real problem. He was the wild hairpin turn in the track you hadn't counted on. And you can run to Des Moines or Peking, for that matter, and you won't be far enough away to escape from that memory. The man has a hold on you, and you might as well admit it.''

Barrie stared at her helplessly. She knew that what Danielle had said was true. As furious as she was with Michael, she hadn't been able to banish him from her mind. His face taunted her every time she closed her eyes. Even her morning shower could not provide safe harbor. The water gliding over her body reminded her of his gentle touch and aroused in her an aching memory.

"Is he back yet?" she asked at last.

"He's due in tonight."

"My, my. You've certainly kept abreast of the latest developments. Do you have his complete itinerary?"

"Nope," Danielle responded cheerfully, refusing to take offense at the taunt. "Just the salient points. Since you refuse to talk to him, I seem to be the next best thing."

"Perhaps you should go out with him, then," Barrie said dryly, though a twinge of jealousy made her practically choke on the suggestion. "You seem to get along well enough, and you're obviously more forgiving than I."

"Sweetie, I'm not about to be second best in anybody's life. And you ought to be thanking your lucky stars that a man like Michael, who is so absolutely perfect for you, seems to think you're better than rum-raisin ice cream."

"I should hope so," Barrie retorted with a grimace.

"I like rum-raisin ice cream."

"Your taste buds have been warped."

"That's beside the point. When Michael gets back here, you ought to see him. The two of you can still work things out, if you'll keep that stubborn pride of yours in check."

Barrie sighed. "We'll see."

Danielle beamed in satisfaction. "Progress at last. I'd better get out of here while I'm still ahead for the day."

"Good idea."

Barrie spent the rest of the day walking the beach under a gray sky that perfectly suited her mood. Danielle had been right about one thing—probably more than one, but it would never do to give her too much credit—she couldn't go on like this. She was not only miserable, she was already bored. She needed to get back to work, and a dress shop in Des Moines or anyplace else was no answer. Deep down she knew that, though the idea had seemed attractively safe and serene for a few fleeting minutes in the emotional aftermath of the cancellation.

Back in her apartment, she pulled out the file cards on which she jotted notes to herself about possible new shows. Sometimes it was only a character description, sometimes a setting, sometimes a business that seemed like a unique backdrop for some crazy characters. As she sorted through them, she began making more notes, chuckling to herself at some of the possibilities, discarding others.

After an hour of examining all the cards several times, she kept coming back to one. The show would feature a successful workaholic father and a career-oriented mother. Their independent teenage kids would be in the throes of rebellion over having spent their entire adolescence cutting grass, cooking dinner and doing the grocery shopping. And, she thought with a wry chuckle, there might be room in this one for a sheepdog.

When the doorbell rang, she was just envisioning the fluffy beast on the kitchen floor as the kids tried to wax around him. Or maybe even tried to use him as a mop. Her heartbeat seemed to stop as the doorbell chimed again. There wasn't a doubt in her mind about who it was. Michael's timing was always impeccable. She was about to create a show with a blasted sheepdog, and he couldn't wait to get his hands on it.

When she opened the door, she stood staring at him silently for a moment. He looked terrible. He was drawn and pale, his eyes red-rimmed from lack of sleep, his cheeks shadowed with the beginning of a beard. Even the dimple in his chin seemed downcast. Despite his appearance, her heart readily flipped over.

"Rough flight?" she asked tartly.

"No. The flight was just fine," he responded wearily, brushing past her. "We have to talk."

"Don't you think we're having this conversation about a week too late?"

"Probably. But the fact remains that since we didn't we're going to have it now." Barrie watched in amazement as he poured himself a glass of Scotch. He must be nervous. She'd never seen him drink anything much stronger than wine.

"For a man who's trying to worm his way back into my good graces, you're being awfully dictatorial," she taunted lightly. "You might want to revise your tactics."

His lips twitched with a tiny smile. "A week ago I was more than willing to be contrite and apologetic. A few days ago I was ready to be charming and win you back. Now you're lucky I don't turn you over my knee and spank you."

Barrie stared at him. He was perfectly serious. She inched a step or two backward and tried to maintain a light, thoughtful tone. "Brute force would be an interesting approach to resolving the problem."

"It works with kids when they get out of line."

"I'm no kid."

"But you've been behaving like one."

Barrie's eyes widened incredulously. "You have the nerve to say that to me after what you've done?"

"I made a lousy mistake of timing, and the one person I care most about in the world got hurt in the process. I'm sorry. I've told you that. I don't know how else to say it. By the time I realized those stories were going into print, it was too late."

"You could have told me when you first made the decision."

"That's just it," he said, running his fingers through his hair nervously. "I didn't make the decision. It was made in New York. I was flying there to try to talk them out of it. I wanted to move the show and give it another chance. I thought the changes you had made..."

"We had made," Barrie murmured distractedly as she focused on what he had just said. It hadn't been his decision at all. He had wanted to save the show.

Knowing that suddenly seemed to make all the difference.

"Whatever. I thought they were working and that the show was finally on the right track. I thought a new time slot would bring in a new audience to sample it."

Barrie sat down next to him, her heart lighter. "You were really going to do that?" she said softly. "You were going to bat for us?"

"I wanted to. I was overruled. And before I could talk to them about the revised schedule I had in mind, the stories broke. By then it was too late."

"Why didn't you tell me that before?"

He stared at her indignantly. "How was I supposed to do that? Leave a message with your answering service?"

"You could have told Danielle."

"I did."

"She never said a word."

"I asked her not to. I told her because I needed her on my side, but I wanted to be the one to tell you myself."

Barrie threw her arms around Michael's neck and hugged him, her lips brushing a kiss across the stubble on his cheek. "Thank you."

"For what?"

"For believing in *Goodbye, Again*."

"I told you from the beginning that I believed in it, just the way I've been telling you that I believe in us."

Barrie took a deep breath and said softly, "You said something like that on the phone the other day. Did you mean it?"

Michael grinned at her wickedly. "You didn't give me the chance to say much. What especially are you referring to?"

She poked him in the ribs. "You know very well what I mean. Don't make me say it."

"Why not? I think you owe me that much for you evident lack of faith. What did I say?"

"Blast you, Michael Compton. You're taking all the romance out of this."

"Out of what?" he taunted innocently.

"Your damn marriage proposal. You asked me to marry you."

"I did? Gee, I must have been in a daze."

"Are you in a daze now?"

"No."

"Well, then?"

"Okay," he relented at last, cupping her chin in his hand and tilting her head until he could look directly into her hopeful brown eyes. "I love you, Barrie MacDonald. Will you marry me?"

She sighed and smiled contentedly. "Yes," she promised. "On one condition."

Michael's brows flew up. "My God, is this going to be anything like negotiating a contract?"

"Something like that."

"Should we call your agent?"

"Oh, I think I can look out for my own interests on this one."

"So what's the condition?"

"That you will never, never say goodbye again."

He grinned at her. "That's going to make it tough to leave for work in the morning."

"Don't go," she suggested, her fingers exploring the inside of his thighs until he moaned softly. "I can keep you occupied."

"We'll be poor."

"We'll be happy."

"We'll be bored."

She looked at him askance and intensified her touch. "Oh, really?"

He groaned. "Forget bored."

"Is it a promise? You'll never leave me again."

"I will never leave you again," he vowed solemnly, his lips hungrily capturing hers.

When his tongue teased against her lips, then dipped inside for a taste of honeyed sweetness, Barrie groaned, too, and melted into Michael's arms. But when his touch became increasingly more intimate as his fingers explored her shoulders, the tips of her breasts, her already throbbing abdomen, she couldn't resist pulling away to note in a prim, shocked tone, "Michael, it is barely eight o'clock. Don't you think you're getting a little carried away for this particular time slot?"

"You're sophisticated enough for what I have in mind at any hour," he retorted dryly. "Besides, we're not on television."

"Thank goodness," Barrie replied, moving back into his embrace.

"Thank goodness," he echoed.

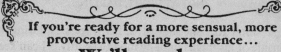

Silhouette Brings You:

Four delightful, romantic stories celebrating the holiday season, written by four of your favorite Silhouette authors.

> **Nora Roberts**—*Home for Christmas*
> **Debbie Macomber**—*Let It Snow*
> **Tracy Sinclair**—*Under the Mistletoe*
> **Maura Seger**—*Starbright*

Each of these great authors has combined the wonder of falling in love with the magic of Christmas to bring you four unforgettable stories to touch your heart.

Indulge yourself during the holiday season . . . or give this book to a special friend for a heartwarming Christmas gift.

Available November 1986

XMAS-1